CAMERON

CAMERON

WILLIAM SHAMBAUGH

DOUBLEDAY & COMPANY, INC.
GARDEN CITY, NEW YORK
1981

All of the characters in this book are fictitious, and any resemblance to actual persons, living or dead, is purely coincidental.

Library of Congress Cataloging in Publication Data

Shambaugh, William.
Cameron.

I. Title.
PS3569.H327C3   813'.54

First Edition

ISBN: 0-385-17589-2   AACR2
Library of Congress Catalog Card Number 81-65661
Copyright © 1981 by William Shambaugh
All Rights Reserved
Printed in the United States of America

CAMERON

CHAPTER 1

He knew he had let himself go. It wasn't something he was proud of, but it had happened.

He could always feel it at this particular hour, when it was almost dark, they were done for the day, and it was an effort to swing the saddle off and carry it over to the corner and just let it fall. He had gotten sloppy, letting things lay where he dropped them, doing only half a job rubbing down his horse, not washing half the time, not running a comb through his hair.

He had let himself go since his wife died. He didn't have to be told. He knew without looking in a mirror. Keep it up, he thought, and he'd end up a crummy old man.

He heard Henry Butler closing the corral but he didn't go out to help him. Henry came into the stable with his horse, lit a lantern and hung it on a nail so he could see what he was doing. Frank put some water where his horse could reach it, wiped his hands on the seat of his pants, coughed, and walked out toward the house.

His instincts, though, hadn't gone completely. He had noticed the two riders up on the ridge, sitting, for more than an hour now. They were suddenly joined by ten or twelve more and were moving slowly down into the valley toward the small ranch.

Henry came out of the stable and said, "You want me to start supper?"

It was just the two of them, and it was just a small place. Frank knew what he had. He didn't fool himself. His wife was dead and his three sons were gone. It was just the two of them left, keeping a few cows busy. Once Henry, when he was young and gullible, had gone down into Mexico on a wild goose chase, a promise of quick money, but he came back three years later and had stuck with Frank ever since. Henry was five years older than Frank and twenty pounds heavier, and had stopped chasing wild geese.

"No," said Frank, "not yet."

"You want me to get a rifle?"

"I don't think it'll help."

"Do you think they'll really do something this time?"

"I don't know."

"He's bringing a lot of help."

Frank smiled. "For two old duffers like us."

"I think I'll get the rifle. No sense making it too easy for them." He started off.

Frank said, "Henry?"

"Yeah."

"This time don't forget to load it."

The riders were closer, moving at a slow but steady pace. There were fourteen of them, he could see now, to be exact. Henry found the rifle in the stable, got it loaded, blew out the lantern, and walked back in the dark. He was tired. He was feeling his age. He was also irritated. He figured his chances of getting supper soon were not good.

The riders came in across the front of the yard and fanned out. They stopped, letting their horses blow a little. They faced the two men on foot in front of them.

Frank for a moment felt a little touch of fear. These men were all young and heavily armed and used to violence. They were used to getting their own way. They were not known for being patient. Frank was aware of a button off his shirt, and the heel was chipped on one of his boots. He wasn't wearing a gun, and didn't even have a belt on. He knew what a joke he must look like to the men sitting easy waiting for Jim Dahlman to get things started.

"Someone get a light, I can't see a thing."

One of the riders struck a match and got a lantern lit. He held it up high sitting on his horse.

"Move out a little so we can see."

He walked his horse out toward Frank and Henry and stopped.

"That's better. My God, this is a crummy place. Why the hell ain't you got something lit up around here?"

Frank didn't say anything.

Jim Dahlman was a big man, over six feet tall, almost forty, successful, hard, ambitious, wealthy, a driver, a schemer. He wore a mustache that drooped at the sides and he kept it trimmed. His teeth were stained with tobacco, but his mustache was trimmed.

"Cameron, I didn't come to talk this time."

Frank turned a little and said, "Henry, the man didn't come to talk. I bet he didn't come to eat either."

"Maybe he's just passing through."

Jim Dahlman said, "I got fifteen hundred head of cattle up on the other side of that ridge."

Frank said, "Well, I got twenty head somewhere between here and the creek."

Dahlman moved quickly; he had his gun out, and he fired a shot into the front of the house. "Cameron, I . . . am . . . done . . . fooling. I ought to put a shot right between your stupid eyes. Do you a favor. I am bringing those cows down through here in the morning."

"That's what the hell you think." Frank couldn't believe he had said it. Even Henry looked over at him.

Dahlman ignored him. He turned in his saddle and said, "All right, take care of the fence, the stable, and the house."

The riders wheeled around and rode off. A couple of them roped the ends of the fence back of the house and pulled out one post after another. A couple rode back to the stable and a fire was started. The two horses inside were turned loose. A man got down to go into the house, striking a match along the wall.

Frank pulled the rifle away from Henry and snapped off a shot that missed. Dahlman fired and hit Frank high in the leg, knocking him flat on his back. He held the gun on Henry.

The big man walked his horse over closer to Frank, thought about it a minute, and said, "Oh, hell, just go. I want you to get out and don't come back."

The house caught on fire. The stable had already blazed up and collapsed. The fence was gone.

The house burned fast. The wood was dry and there wasn't that much to it. Dahlman wheeled his horse around and they were gone.

Henry hunkered down and checked Frank's leg. He said, "I'll get the horses and get you into town."

Frank lay back, his eyes closed, his teeth clenched. He took a couple of deep breaths. "Jesus, that hurts."

"Hold on."

"Henry, I'll tell you what."

"What?"

"You lay down here and bleed, and I'll go get the horses."

Doc Kruger finished with the bandage and went over to the sink to wash his hands. Frank lay stretched out on the table. He still had his shirt and vest on but his pants had been pulled off and dumped into the corner. A huge bandage was wrapped around his upper leg. He lay with his eyes closed, pale, breathing just a little easier now. He wiped away the perspiration on his forehead. He still didn't open his eyes. He could smell the dirt and sweat on himself, and the alcohol and witch hazel in the room. He was nowhere near ready to move yet.

Henry sat in a corner of the small room and tried to stay out of the way. He said, quietly, "What do you think, Doc?"

Doc Kruger finished at the sink. He sipped from a water glass that contained better whiskey than was found in the saloon. He unrolled his sleeves. He was a short, small, dapper man.

"He's finished. He can go. You can take him home now."

"How's his leg?"

"Right now it's not as good as the other one. It may never be again. But it'll get better. About six months from now."

"Nothin's broke?"

"A lot of muscle has been shot to hell. A lot of blood has been lost. But no, nothing has been broken."

"Can he walk on it?"

"Sure." He smiled slightly. "But I don't think he'll want to."

"Can he ride?"

"He better not."

"If he's careful?"

"He'll start to bleed. He can't afford to do that. He did enough of that with you getting him in here. Take him home. Put him to bed, at least for a week."

Frank, with his eyes still closed, said, "Doc. I think we got a problem." He didn't try to sit up. He didn't open his eyes. But he said, "Henry, get my pants."

Henry stepped over to him and looked down. "Frank, you need more than a pair of pants."

"I know. We'll start with the pants. Get them. I'll get them on."

"Then what?"

"Then I'm going to stand up. And then, more than likely, I'll fall back down." He opened his eyes and let out a deep breath. "Jesus, Henry, you got to take life as it is. And right now, this is all we got."

"You standing up and falling down? That don't seem like much to me."

Doc Kruger came over to Frank. He said, "I'll help." Before Frank knew what he was doing, Kruger had his arm behind Frank's neck and with a deft move swung him up and around so his feet were dangling down from the table and Frank was sitting up. And suddenly sweating, suddenly swooning. Just as smoothly, Doc Kruger handed him the water glass and Frank finished it off in one long swallow.

He had his eyes closed again and he said, between deep breaths, "Doc, promise me one thing?"

"What?"

"If anyone ever shoots you in the leg, I get first crack at fixing you up."

Doc Kruger said to Henry, "Get a wagon and lay him in that and take him home."

"I can't do that."

Frank said, "What he's trying to say is, Jim Dahlman is the one who shot me."

"I don't believe that."

"You don't?"

"No. If Jim Dahlman had shot you, it would have been dead center."

"He was having a bad day. Look, he shot me, don't worry about that. He shot me, burned down my house and stable and tore down my fence. He was not in a good mood."

"I take it he was trying to tell you something."

"I wouldn't sell, so he foreclosed. I don't think it would be a good idea for me to go back there."

Henry got his pants and helped him pull them on. Frank slowly slid off the table and stood on one foot. He leaned back against the table and pulled his Bull Durham sack from his vest pocket and fished a piece of paper from another pocket and rolled a cigarette. He lit it and drew on it deeply a moment, taking his time.

He said to Doc Kruger, slowly exhaling the smoke, "I got to ride, bleed or not. I got to go somewhere, and I better not take a week doing it."

"You suit yourself."

Frank looked at him steadily for a minute, enjoying the smoke, then said, "It's not going to work, though, is it?"

"No, it's not."

"I didn't think so."

"Let me make a suggestion."

"Be my guest."

"There's a dugout about eight miles from here. I was out there the other day. There's a woman living there, a half-breed, part Kiowa. She don't talk to anyone but me. There's a young girl with her. She adopted her somewhere along the way. The two of them live there and no one goes near the place, and if you get out there, I think you could stay there until your leg heals."

"A dugout?"

"It is not much but . . ."

Frank looked at him, finished the cigarette and said, "Yeah, I know. Neither am I."

He knew it would be bad. He had taken it into account. But he hadn't figured far enough. The ride out was sheer hell. His leg throbbed. He was starting to run a temperature. He had a headache. He needed a drink of water. He needed to relieve himself. When the wagon finally stopped, he considered getting Henry to finish the job.

Henry climbed down and said, "I'll be right back."

It was dark. There were few stars in the sky. He was getting the chills.

Henry came back with a woman, Jesus, who Frank thought looked even worse than he did. They got him out of the wagon. She was strong. He could make out a dugout cut into the side of a bank. A buffalo skin hung down in place of a door. A young girl about seventeen held it open.

They carried him toward it. He clenched his teeth, sweating like a horse. Hell, he thought, he had gotten all the way from the wagon to the door without yelling once, or trying to choke either one of them carrying him. Maybe things were looking up.

There was just one room. A candle was burning on a small table. It was warm inside. They got him on what passed for a bed. He lost track of where the woman was. The young girl had curled up on something in one of the corners and sat there watching him.

Henry leaned over. "The arrangements are made. I paid her for one month. One month should make a difference."

"Henry. I'm not staying here a month."

"I didn't say that. I said I paid her for a month. That's just in case."

"In case what?"

"In case you do stay here a month." Henry stood up. "Take care of yourself."

"Where are you going?"

Henry walked to the door. He looked back. "I'm going for the boys," he said, and left.

CHAPTER 2

Kate Miller saw the older man come in first. He carried a rifle in his hand. He looked around and then motioned the younger man in next, his hands handcuffed in front of him. The younger man was motioned to sit on a bench against the wall and wait.

She stood near the trestle table at the far end of the stage station, bringing coffee from the kitchen. A squatter and his family were just finishing supper. A drummer sat on a bench away from the door, waiting with a suitcase for the stage.

The older man, Curley Buchanan, looked back, uneasy, at the young man who sat quiet, hat brim pulled down, hands still. He came across the room. "When's the next stage?"

Kate said, "Which way?"

"Either way."

"About an hour."

"Give me a ticket."

"Harley will be in in a minute. He's checking the horses. He runs this place. I just cook the meals." She was thirty at least, probably more, but still not bad looking. A little hard, but with a figure, and she took care of her hair.

The door opened and a tall, slender man came in carrying a horse blanket. He put it behind a battered, wooden desk that had no chair. An overturned barrel stood behind it. He wore a coat that he took off. He made himself look busy.

Curley said, "You Harley?"

"Yes."

"I want one ticket."

Harley looked at the rifle and then noticed a badge pinned on the shirt under Curley's vest. He looked over at the young man sitting on the bench. He saw the handcuffs. He noticed he had no gun.

"Just one?"

"Just one."

"What about him?"

"It's for him. He's the one going. I'm staying."

"Who is he?"

"He didn't say."

"What'd he do?"

"He shot Purcell Pomeroy. He claims Purcell palmed a card."

"Purcell Pomeroy? The dealer over at Three Trees? I thought Purcell was good."

"He was. He sat in that same chair for five years and nobody ever saw him palm a card before."

"That's what I heard."

"Well, apparently that man over there is just as good at his business as Purcell was at his."

"What's that?"

"Shooting people who palm cards when he's playing."

Harley went behind the desk. Kate moved to get a better look at the young man. He was of medium build, maybe a little slender, with light hair. He sat still, indifferent to what was happening.

She walked over. "You want supper?"

He moved his head up just enough to look at her. He took his time. "No." It was spoken softly.

"Coffee?"

He considered that. He stood up. Curley jumped, raising the rifle. His nerves were bad. "What the hell you doing?"

Morgan Cameron stood still. He said, evenly, "Just getting a cup of coffee."

"Well, let me know the next time. *Before* you move. Okay, okay, go get the damn thing."

Morgan went over to the edge of the kitchen and waited. Kate poured coffee into a cup and handed it to him. She stood close, her leg brushing against him. He raised the cup with both hands and sipped a little.

The squatter said, "If you'd like some supper, there's plenty of room here. The kids can move over. You're more'n welcome."

"No, thanks. The coffee's enough." He looked at Kate and walked back.

Curley went out, came back in, and set a bedroll down beside Morgan. He said, "You remember the deal?"

"I remember."

"There's no second thoughts?"

"No."

Curley was nervous. He pulled the ticket out of his

pocket and handed it to Morgan. "Okay. I figure you got about forty-five minutes. I can't stay."

"I know."

"I need your word."

"I already gave that to you."

"I had nothing to do with this. You know that, don't you? I'm just doing what I was told to do."

"I know that."

Curley dug a key out of his vest pocket. He hesitated, and swallowed a couple of times. He checked the time.

Morgan said, "It's all right."

"What?"

Morgan held out his hands. "It'll be all right. I'll keep the bargain."

Curley took the key, unlocked the handcuffs, and put them in his belt. He didn't move for a moment. Morgan didn't rub his wrists. He simply lowered his hands to his lap and sat still.

Curley stood up. "I reckon I'll go. It's getting late."

Morgan didn't say anything.

Curley backed off, keeping his rifle pointed to the floor. He got to the door. Harley came around the desk.

"Hey. What's going on?"

"Nothing."

"You took the cuffs off him."

"I know I did."

"You brought him in here with both hands handcuffed. If that's the way you brought him in, that's the way he stays until he goes out."

"You want him handcuffed, here, you do it. I'm leaving."

"Wait a minute."

"You got any complaints, you make them to Sheriff Calder. I am simply following his orders. He said bring this man over here, buy him a ticket on the *first* stage, give him the ticket, take off the cuffs, and come on back. Now that's what I'm doing."

"I don't want him in here."

"He ain't going to bother no one. He gave his word. We said we'd buy the ticket and take off the cuffs, and he said he'd take the stage and he wouldn't bother no one."

"And you believe that?"

"I do. If you don't, you tell him." Then Curley stepped out the door and was gone.

No one moved. Morgan Cameron sipped the coffee and looked at the floor. Kate walked over with the coffeepot. She refilled his cup.

"Did you really shoot Purcell Pomeroy?"

"That was yesterday."

The squatter and his family finished eating and moved away from the table. He was a short, stocky man. His wife looked tired. They had two children about nine and ten. They moved over onto a long bench against the wall near the drummer, dragging three large suitcases held together with some old rope. The man seemed gentle with the children.

Harley went back behind the desk. He fussed with

some papers, licking the end of a blunt pencil and making some notes. He didn't look over at Morgan.

The drummer opened his sample case and rooted around until he came up with a cigar. He wore a derby hat that he now pushed back while he got the cigar going.

Kate said, "I got some pie in the kitchen."

Morgan said, "I better sit still."

"Come on. I could use some conversation with someone for a change who isn't trying to steal something, sell something, or grab something."

"I make people nervous when I move around."

She gave him a direct look. "They get nervous anyway. Come on. You only got maybe a half hour. What kind of trouble can you get into in thirty minutes?"

"Maybe next time I come through."

"There may not be any pie then."

"I promised I'd sit still."

"I'm not asking you to dance."

He looked at her. She was good looking. He said, "Maybe I . . ."

The door opened. Three men came in. They were heavily armed. They walked over to the middle of the room and dropped the saddles and bedrolls they were carrying on the floor. They were loud, wearing large Spanish spurs, two of them in leather chaps. They carried rifles and wore handguns and had knives in their belts. They took a good look around the room.

Kurt Mandee, the biggest of the bunch, was starting to run a little to fat. He had big shoulders, and a big, gruff face that needed a shave. He wore his bandana tied behind his neck. He had on a leather vest that had seen its best days, and you could see heavy underwear under his shirt. He took up a lot of space.

He said to Harley, "When's the next stage due?" He talked loud.

Harley stayed behind the desk. "About a half hour."

"Good." He turned away.

"You want tickets?"

Kurt looked back. "You talking to me?"

"I was wondering if you wanted tickets?"

"If I want something, I'll tell you."

Another of the three, with a full beard and red hair, went over and sat down behind the table. He sat at the end by the squatter's family. The squatter called one boy over closer to him on the bench.

The last of them was an old man with teeth missing, carrying an old Hawken rifle. He sat down at the near end of the table.

Kurt looked at Kate. He said, "You got some coffee?"

"Maybe."

"Well, sister, why don't you find three cups and some coffee and put it on that table, and why don't you do that right now."

She looked at Morgan, but he had slipped back down under his hat. She turned and went out into the kitchen.

Morgan knew it was going to take a little luck. He had seen too many Kurt Mandees. They brought trouble with them. They were constantly asking for it. Morgan was thirty, which wasn't bad. He was still quick and strong, but it was fifteen years since he had been home and there had been a lot of Kurt Mandees along the way.

He had been happy at home. He left because he was restless. He wanted to see what there was to see. His pa had said, "Go take a look. We'll be here if you want to come back." His mother hadn't said anything. But when he opened his bedroll the first night away, he found a small gold watch that had belonged to his grandfather, and he knew that she had put it there. His one regret in fifteen years was that he hadn't been able to get home when she died.

His brother Reuben was the oldest by two years and had left home the year before, but his brother Tom was two years younger and was still at home, so his pa had some help. Morgan headed due west for California first, taking his time, picking up an odd job here and there when he had to, making his way through the gold mines, going as far north as San Francisco and watching the best gamblers ply their trade. He stood off to the side and watched everyone for a couple of years, listening and learning. He stayed in the background, watching how other people did things, seeing how dumb some men were and how smart other men were.

He bought a deck of cards when he was eighteen. He started practicing by himself. He would deal out four hands and play each one and notice how things tended to go. He learned what you could usually expect in each situation.

It was at that time also that he found out he had a natural touch with a gun. He had practiced as a boy when his pa wasn't looking, and now things just fell into place. He was quick and could hit just about anything he wanted to. So he practiced that, too, when he was alone. He didn't let it show.

He played his first card game when he was twenty. He waited more than two hours behind a table before he had the nerve to sit down. The dealer was an older man, laconic, patient, thorough. Morgan lost, but it took seven hours for it to happen.

He didn't lose the next time. The dealer asked him his name before he left the table. He hesitated; he liked it better when no one knew he was around, when he could hang on the edge of things and watch and no one noticed him. But he was also satisfied with himself. He had played well. He said softly, "Morgan Cameron."

The dealer said, "Jason Motter." And he offered Morgan a cigar.

Morgan left town the next day. He drifted around for a while, never staying too long in one place. He continued to gamble, gaining experience, getting better, but never thinking of himself as a gambler. He always thought he'd eventually settle down working cows on a ranch somewhere. Right now he still had places he wanted to see.

He traveled east, looking forward to seeing some of the great riverboats. He made several trips up and down the river, playing cards, looking at the land, taking a look at some of the cities. He still practiced when he was alone, both with the cards and his gun, and he was gaining poise and confidence. He left the Mississippi and went to

Texas, crossed the Rio Grande, and took a look at Mexico. And killed his first man.

It was late and it was raining, and he found a cantina in a small town and went in looking for a dry place and some warm food. There were about fifteen people standing at the bar and sitting at the tables, talking in low tones, running out the last of the night. There were a few Americans.

In a far corner, a man sat by himself. He was in his late forties. He was eating, and seemed tired. No one attempted any conversation with him. He looked like a Texan. A woman came over and sat with him. They didn't talk. She was dark and pretty.

Morgan found a table at the other end of the room. A heavy-set woman came over; he talked to her and she brought him some chili, bread, and some whiskey. He didn't drink much, but it took the chill away.

The door burst open. Six men pushed in and fanned out through the room. Three of them were Mexicans, three were Texans. The leader was a big man, a Texan wearing a Mexican sombrero. He spotted the man sitting in the corner and went over after him.

"Look what we got here. Someone told me you were a smart man, Hawk. I don't know if I believe it now."

The seated man held a spoon in one hand and a piece of bread in the other. He held them still. He didn't move.

The other man said, "Someone told me you want to find the Hawk. You just hang around the cantina in Los Polos and you'll see him. He'll come to see Dolores Llaydos. I

told him the Hawk is not that dumb. Jesus, you learn
something new every day."

"Spurgeon," the seated Texan spoke, quietly, slowly,
but emphatically, "no."

"No?"

"No. Not now."

"I've been looking for you for two months. I don't intend to spend two more."

The Texan continued to look at Spurgeon but he said,
"Dolores, go home." He sounded very sad.

She didn't move.

He said, "I'll come over later."

She still didn't move. Morgan could see she was crying,
but he couldn't hear her. The six men were all facing the
table and waiting. Spurgeon spat some tobacco on the
floor.

The Texan said, "I want to take her home first." It
seemed to take a lot of effort.

"No."

"I'll be right back."

"No, damn it! You don't get to do nothing, except what
I say. And I say I got you this time."

"You don't have anything." He held the spoon and the
bread and looked right at Spurgeon. The big man almost
took a step back. Then Morgan noticed the sweat on
Spurgeon's back, and could see how tense he was.

Again, the Texan said, softly, with intensity, "Dolores,
go home."

She shook her head.

"It will be easier for me."

She shook her head again. The tears were running down her face.

"Spurgeon." There was a note of hard desperation in his voice. "I am going to take her home first."

"You ain't going nowhere. And the only place she's going is with us when we're done." He grinned.

Morgan at first didn't even realize he had done it. He stood up, stepped out away from the table and said, "Hawk, you ready to go?"

Everyone jumped, and looked back nervously. Morgan was behind the six, just standing there. He said, "It's getting late. Why don't we go?"

The Texan looked at him. Spurgeon turned slightly, trying to keep his eyes on the Texan and yet peering back through the room to see who it was. He took a good look. Morgan wasn't imposing; he looked young, and he wasn't holding a gun. Spurgeon wasn't that worried, but he hesitated. It altered the situation.

The Texan said, "Spurgeon. I'm going to get up. I'm going to get up and take her home."

"No! No, damn it, no!" His face was red. He was taking deep breaths.

The Texan said, "Son, if you could just keep the two to my left busy, I'd appreciate it."

"Sure."

Before Morgan could think, the Texan had dropped the bread and spoon. He was in a half crouch, moving away from the girl, firing a gun. Spurgeon didn't get his gun out. He was hit first. The room exploded.

Without thinking, just as he had practiced, Morgan drew his gun and fired, looking right at the Mexican near the wall, at the Texan's far left. He saw him go down, but he had already fired at the man next to him. Someone fired a rifle. People rushed for the door. Two jumped over the bar and fell to the floor.

The firing stopped as suddenly as it had started. Both men Cameron had fired at were dead. Spurgeon was dead. One Mexican sat against a wall holding his side. The other two were dead. The Texan was standing up, holding his gun, but he had been hit in the side. The girl was pulling up his shirt, trying to see.

The Texan said, "I appreciate your help."

"That's all right."

"Which way are you headed?"

"Nowhere in particular."

"Are you in a hurry?"

"No."

"If you could wait until tomorrow, I'm heading for New Mexico. I wouldn't mind company."

Morgan thought it over. It took him five seconds. "I never saw New Mexico before."

The girl held some cloth against the wound. The Texan looked at it; it wasn't bad. He said to Morgan, "I don't think I could have done this without you."

Standing close to him, Morgan wasn't too sure of that. The Texan said, "You don't mind company, do you?"

Morgan shook his head no. Right then he was ready to follow him anywhere.

They stayed together three years. They spent some time scouting for the U. S. Army, and Cameron learned a lot about the Apache. One thing he learned was, if he wanted to reach thirty, he'd better get a job doing something else.

Then the Texan took a job as sheriff in Tombstone. Morgan went with him, but it wasn't the kind of thing he cared for, so he left after a year. It was not an easy decision to make.

Over that time, they spent a lot of time talking. Morgan grew up. He always remembered something the Texan had said about life: At best, it's short, no matter how long you live. So enjoy the sunsets you see, the food you eat, and the times you keep company with a good woman. It comes to an end, sooner or later, for all of us. Don't waste any more than you have to.

Morgan wasn't enjoying what he was doing, so he did what the Texan would have done in his place: he left. He heard a year later, sitting in a card game in Cheyenne, that the sheriff in Tombstone had been shot in the back by a drunk with a shotgun. He finished the hand, then went to his room and went to bed early. He didn't feel like doing much of anything else all of a sudden.

Over the years, he picked up a reputation and a certain style. He stayed on the move. He wasn't happy and he wasn't unhappy, he just made do wherever he was. If it was bad enough, he'd get his horse and go somewhere else.

He tried to keep his mistakes to a minimum. He was fairly successful until the night he played cards in Three

Trees and caught the dealer palming cards and shot him. He had called him and got the two of them in a situation that could end only one way. He should have simply quit and left. Shooting him was dumb. He didn't usually do dumb things.

CHAPTER 3

Kurt Mandee drank his coffee standing in the middle of the room, looking around. He couldn't sit still. He had to assert himself. He looked at the drummer.

"What do you got in that suitcase?"

"Just samples."

"I figured that. What kind of samples?"

"Gloves. I got work gloves, leather gloves, most of them . . ."

"Open it up."

"What?"

"Open up the suitcase."

The drummer looked around. Harley kept his nose in his papers. He was not going to be any help. The drummer coughed nervously and put the suitcase on the bench and opened it up.

Mandee began poking through the samples, pulling out gloves, trying them on, putting them back, and he said, "Give my friends a pair. Just like these."

"What size do they wear?"

"They'll show you."

The drummer carried a couple of pairs over to the table. The man with the red hair didn't look up. He kept eating. But the old man with the missing teeth snapped, "Just put them down. I'll take them all. That other pair you got in your hands, leave that here, too."

"They run a quarter a piece. That's five pairs there."

"I ain't buying. You're donating. Ain't that what he's doing, Mandee?" He cackled a little.

"Sure. Ain't that what you're doing, drummer?"

"I guess I could give you one pair free."

The man with the red hair said, "Sit down."

The drummer glanced nervously over at Mandee. His cigar had gone out. He left the gloves on the table and went back to the bench and sat down.

Mandee held up his cup and said, "More coffee."

Kate came to the kitchen door and said, "There's the pot. You can get it yourself."

"If I were you, sister, I'd fill this cup."

She gave him a hard look. She said, "I don't sell gloves."

He looked at her, then changed his mind, laughed, and said, "Tough as nails, huh? Well, sister, we'll see. Maybe before I go."

He walked over and filled the cup, turned, and came back across the room. He walked over close to Morgan and put one foot up on the bench. He said, softly, "You look funny sitting over here, friend. You don't have a gun. Not where I can see one anyway."

Morgan didn't say anything.

"I get the feeling you're waiting for the stage. That's the only thing on your mind."

Morgan still didn't say anything.

"I also get the feeling you know how to mind your own business."

Morgan didn't move.

Mandee said, "I ain't going to bother you, and I don't want you to bother me. The old man wanted to sit over there where he could point that damn Hawken rifle right at you, but I told him there was no need for that. You and me, we understand each other. It's going to be live and let live. Right, friend?"

Morgan didn't say anything and he didn't look up.

Mandee turned and said to Harley, "Where the hell is that stage? What are you running here?"

Harley jumped. He made a big show out of consulting his watch. He said, "It's due anytime now. It could be running a little late, but it's due."

"Yeah." Mandee turned and went across the room again. He walked over close to the squatter. He stared at the woman. She looked away. She was pretty in a plain manner, and seemed tired. It was obvious she had a nice figure.

He leaned down and said to her, "What's your name?"

She looked at her husband.

"Lady, I asked you what's your name."

She didn't answer.

He looked at her husband and said, "What's her name?"

The squatter didn't look at him. He said, in a low voice, "We don't want no trouble."

"Nobody's giving you trouble. I just want to know her name."

The squatter looked up for a moment and then away. He said, "Why don't you leave us alone? We're not bothering you."

"Hey, friend. All I want to know is what her name is."

The squatter didn't say anything. He sat with his arm around his one son, sitting up against him.

Mandee sat down beside the woman. She jumped and started to move away but he held her by the arm. He said, "What's your name?" He loomed over her. She could smell the tobacco on him. She was terrified.

Her husband suddenly said, "Gladys." His face was flushed.

"Now we're getting somewhere. Now we're getting some cooperation."

"You know her name, now let her go."

"I don't know how you nesters do it, but you got some good looking women." He got up, walked over to the squatter, and said, "Friend, you haven't been following things too well. This trip to Fleetwood is long and boring. I just picked me a seat partner. Someone to keep me company. When the stage comes, she gets on, you stay off. You wait for the next one. I want her undivided attention."

The squatter said, flatly, "Just leave us alone."

Mandee stood very close and said, "Look, dirt pusher, when that stage gets here, she gets on and you stay off. You understand me?"

Kate walked over. "Let them alone. They . . ."

Mandee whirled, furious, and said, "No! You didn't want to pour coffee, I don't want to hear any advice!"

"I'm giving it to you anyway. Let them alone."

"Lady, you might as well go back in the kitchen and wash some dishes because she's getting on that stage and he's staying off."

She turned. "Harley, you hear what he's doing?"

Harley got up and walked outside.

She looked at the old man. He just cackled and said, "Just watch out I don't decide to take you along, too."

The man with the red hair finished eating, sat back and pulled out his Bull Durham sack to make a cigarette.

She went over to Morgan. "Are you just going to sit there?"

He didn't move.

She said, "Do you just shoot gamblers?"

He still didn't move.

She sat down beside him and raised his hat until he had to look at her. "Are you really going to let him do this?"

"It has nothing to do with me."

"That's a crock and you know it."

"Do you get worked up like this very often?"

"Every day."

"I can't afford it."

"Listen to me. Don't let this happen."

He looked away.

"You're not going to do anything?"

"No. Nothing." He tilted the hat back down.

Harley came in the door and said, "The stage's coming. There'll be a ten minute layover, then we'll load up."

They could hear the horses now, and the stage coming closer. Finally it swung into the yard in front of the station, and they could hear the driver talking the horses to a stop, getting them to stand still while they were being unhitched. Harley said again, "Ten minutes," and went back outside.

Two older men came in, neither one wearing a gun, and headed for the table for coffee. An older woman carrying a parasol came in and tried to find a clean spot at the table.

Then an older man came in. He had a beard and a chew in his mouth. He was heavyset and his clothes had seen their best day. One of the pockets on his vest was torn and hung loose. He looked around carefully. He stared at the man with the hat over his eyes for a minute, then walked over and said, "Morgan?"

Morgan moved his head slowly, just enough to see the man in front of him. "Jesus Christ." He said it softly.

"Morgan Cameron?"

The man with the red hair sat up and looked over.

Morgan pushed his hat back. "Henry. It's been fifteen years."

"I know. You look good."

"What are you doing here?"

"Looking for you."

"I think you found me."

"Your pa needs you."

"What's wrong?"

"They took the ranch away from him."

"He wouldn't let them do that."

"Not when you were living at home. But things have

changed since your mother died. He's let himself go a lot. He needs some help."

Morgan stood up. "Well, then I reckon I'll go home."

Harley stuck his head in the door and yelled, "It's time. Let's load up."

The squatter reached for his suitcases. He said to his sons, "Let's go." He didn't look at Mandee.

Mandee stepped over in front of him. The old man with the missing teeth moved away from the table a little, cradling the rifle in his arms. The man with the red hair stayed at the table, but moved farther into the corner. He didn't take his eyes off Morgan. Kate stood at the kitchen door.

Morgan said to Henry, "Hand me that war bag."

Henry handed it to him and he opened it and took out a gun. He swung the belt around and strapped it on. It was done smoothly, easily, quickly.

The man with the red hair said, "Kurt."

"What?" He was just about to say something to the squatter.

"That man over there is Morgan Cameron."

"I don't know no Morgan Cameron."

"He was with the Hawk in Tombstone."

Mandee shifted a little. "The Hawk?"

"Yeah. There was a Morgan Cameron with the Hawk at Tombstone for a while. I've heard some say he was better."

Mandee turned and looked at Morgan. He noticed the gun. He said, "Is that true?"

"I was at Tombstone once."

"No. Are you better than the Hawk?"

"That's not true."

"Well, you better be, friend, if you're gonna keep that gun on."

The squatter said to his wife, "Come on, Let's go."

She stood up and took the one boy's hand.

Mandee didn't look at him but he said, "Nester, sit down."

The old man with the missing teeth swung the rifle up and pointed it at Morgan. He said, "I ain't missed a shot like this in twenty years."

Mandee turned, found the squatter, and said, "I told you, she's getting on and you're staying off."

The squatter said, "No."

Mandee said, "The first one I shoot is that kid there, and then that one, and then the woman."

Kate started into the room.

Morgan said, "No. Stay in the kitchen."

She stopped.

The old man with the missing teeth said, "Jesus, Kurt, let's go."

Mandee reached for the woman.

Morgan said, very softly, "Mandee."

The man with the red hair raised both hands slowly and placed them palms down on the table in full view. He looked at Morgan and said, "I'm passing."

Henry was standing at Morgan's right. He said, "Do you want me to shoot this old geezer if he shoots you, Morgan?"

It was just enough to distract the old man. He looked at

Henry for a brief moment, and Morgan drew and fired, driving him off his feet. The rifle went off, blowing a hole in the ceiling.

Morgan shot Mandee in the same easy motion. The outlaw had pulled his gun, but hadn't been able to fire it yet.

Kate flew out of the kitchen and got the two kids and the woman out through the door and up onto the stage. The squatter took his time, staring down at Mandee. He walked around him without changing his expression.

He held out his hand to Morgan and said, "Thank you."

Kate was waiting for Morgan when he came out. She stood close to him and said, "Boy, you took your good old time getting around to it."

"You got a point." He thought she was pretty.

"However, when you did get around to it, I can't complain about the results."

He just looked at her. He didn't know what to do.

She said, "I don't expect you'll get back this way again too soon."

"No, I don't expect I will."

"That's the way my luck runs. If you ever do, though, I'll have a piece of pie for you."

He surprised himself. He touched her and said, "I don't know how things will go, but if I get the chance, I'll come back to see you."

She suddenly kissed him. She said, "I haven't kissed a man like you in a long time, and I don't know if I ever will again." She stepped back and said, fiercely, "Try."

Then she went back inside.

CHAPTER 4

Reuben Cameron got up slowly, taking his time. He reached for his hat before he pulled on his boots. He rolled up his bedroll and put it with his saddle.

It would not be light for another twenty minutes. He stirred up the fire and heated some coffee. He got his breakfast ready and glanced down the long slope from the trees to where the train sat. The grading crews were starting to move around. Some lanterns were lit, and the cooks were busy in the kitchen car. He preferred sleeping alone away from the train. He had told Jack Casemont he would hunt buffalo for them, but he wouldn't sleep with them. Jack had said, "I don't blame you, I'm fussy who I sleep with, too." Jack's brother, Don, had said, "The hell you are."

The Union Pacific had started laying rails at Omaha, heading west. At first they laid a mile a day but that pace had already increased to two. Reuben had come down out of the mountains and signed on to supply buffalo meat for the work crews.

He finished breakfast, cleaned up, saddled his horse, and started down toward the railroad camp. Out in front on the tracks stood the flatcar holding 700-pound rails.

The tracks ended sixty feet in front of it. Up ahead, grading crews worked to level the roadbed, dropping ties on it after it was smoothed out. Iron crews would pull the rails from the flatcar and put them down on the ties with such precision that the spikers and clampers wouldn't have to move them to fasten them in place.

Behind the flatcar stood close to twenty other cars—carpenter's shop, feed store, wash house, sleeping cars, eating cars, kitchen, telegrapher's car, supply car, and a number of private coaches.

He paused for a moment halfway down the slope. It was light now, and the work crews were moving away from the kitchen and sleeping cars. Noise started up as they began working. Steam was built up in the engine at the rear end of the train. Rails were dropped, spikes were driven home, and the sound of voices carried up away from the roadbed.

Reuben got a plug of tobacco out of his vest pocket and bit off a chew. He wore a sweeping mustache and a Colt .45. He also carried a Sharps rifle. He rode a huge bay, strong, not that fast, but it could go all day. He sat a moment and let his soul pull together. Then, when he was ready, he rode in all the way.

He came in through the shanty town that attached itself to the train. As they moved west, the railroaders were happy to see that they were followed by a movable crowd of gamblers, peddlers, and prostitutes. The easy money also attracted gunfighters, saloonkeepers, and thieves, and they too kept pace with the railroad every step of the way.

They were not up this early. They slept while the rails were being laid. At night the place would be crawling with women, gandy dancers, teamsters, soldiers, and gamblers, moving around huge bonfires, drinking and gambling.

Clayton Roberts stood near the kitchen car and watched Reuben ride in. As unit foreman, he controlled everything that moved once the workday started. He reported only to Jack Casemont. He was just forty and had been with railroads since he was fourteen. He had never been West before, but he had laid track around Pittsburgh for years and could crack heads with anyone. He stopped drinking when he was thirty-five, but it hadn't sweetened his disposition at all. He watched Reuben come in and thought, he don't say much but there's one man I wouldn't want to upset.

Clayton stood on the steps of the car and said, "Reuben."

Reuben stopped his horse, shifted his chew, and said, "Clayton."

"You ready to go out?"

"Yeah. How many do you want?"

"Get me six today."

"All right."

"And listen. Meryl Baker said he seen some Indian signs. How about making a sweep before you come in and tell me what you think."

"I told you what I thought when he said that the other day."

"I know. But take a look for me, will you?"

"You don't have to worry until we get closer to Cheyenne."

"Meryl said he saw some signs when he came in yesterday."

"Meryl Baker is a horse's ass."

"Reuben, the man worked for Crook as a scout for years. He must know something."

"I knew Baker when he was at Fort Sills. He couldn't find his own pants if he had them on." He looked at Clayton and said, flatly, "I wouldn't have him work for me if he came for nothing."

Clayton held up his hand. He had a habit of ticking off his points on his fingers. He said, "First, Jack hired him. Second, he was hired to scout. Third, he said he saw signs. So, there I am. Take a look for me."

"You hired me to shoot buffalo. You hired him to scout."

"I know what I hired you to do. Reuben, damnit, as a favor, take a look before you come in."

Clayton had always been fair with him. He nodded. He pulled his horse around and said, "I take a look everytime." He looked back over his shoulder as he rode away, almost smiled, and said, "This time I'll tell you what I see."

Reuben rode over and picked up the skinners and their wagons. They followed him out of camp, out across the plains. The sound of rails being laid behind them was steady, a persistent rhythm.

Reuben was the oldest and the first to leave home. He was not quite twenty at the time. He simply said one night at supper, "I think I'll go take a look around."

His father said, "Around where?"

"I ain't never been anywhere, so I guess everywhere would be a good place to start."

"When?"

"Tomorrow."

"Before or after breakfast?"

"Before."

Frank Cameron knew these things happened, but for twenty years not one member of his family had ever been more than a half hour away. He wasn't ready for it. He didn't want his son to go, but he would have died before he would say that to him. He had left his own home when he had been seventeen; he had loved his mother and father, and yet he was thrilled to be on his own. So he drank his coffee and said, "If you get the chance, come back sometime and tell us what you saw."

Reuben's mother hadn't said anything. But that night she came in and covered him with an extra blanket. She thought he was asleep, so she kissed him before she slipped out. She hadn't done that since he was ten. He reached up in the dark and felt his cheek, felt how wet it was, and knew she had been crying. It wasn't easy to fall back to sleep.

He headed for the mountains. He didn't know how green he was. He knew a lot about cows and breaking horses, but he didn't know anything about people.

He came to a ferry crossing just as it was getting dark

about two weeks after he had left home. The river was swift at that point. He could see the mountains on the other side. It was too difficult for a horse to swim. Everyone used the ferry. A rough building stood just back from the water, serving as a combination saloon and general store. Lamps were lit inside. The bar was inside the door and there was a kitchen around back with only a half-roof. An old man with his two sons and a daughter ran the place.

There were seven horses tied along the rail when Reuben rode in. Three men were sitting at a table eating and four were standing at the bar. Reuben hesitated at the door. He felt uncomfortable. He told the old man he didn't drink and had cooked his own supper; all he wanted was a way across the river. If the ferry wasn't running anymore that night, did he know of another crossing up or down the river?

The old man laughed and said, "Hell, you don't want to go looking up *or* down the river for another crossing." He'd take him across right now, if that's what he wanted, although he was more than welcome to spend the night right there. Elsie could show him a place to bed down. He sized Reuben up, pulled off his apron, and yelled for one of his boys to pour drinks awhile. He got a lantern and took Reuben's arm and led him outside. He walked with a limp but he had a lot of energy, and soon he got the boy and his horse down to the river and up on the ferry and he pushed off. They were soon halfway out in the river.

"Come here, son," he said, "and hold this damn tiller for me while I fix a chew. Jesus, it's cold."

Reuben walked back and reached for the tiller. The old man slipped behind him and suddenly Reuben felt his side burn. He doubled over and saw the old man pull a knife out of him; then felt the old man stripping him of his money and bag and gun. Finally, he was flipped over the side and into the water.

The current was swift, and he was pulled under and away from the ferry and downstream. He came up and went under again and his side hurt and he felt sick and had to force himself to struggle.

Finally he managed to get out of the water, to pull himself up on the bank. It was dark. He was miles below the ferry. He had no horse and he was still bleeding. He was wet and cold. He didn't know where he was.

He pushed himself to his feet. He decided to go inland, away from the river, in case someone came looking for his body. He didn't know when he passed out.

When he came to it was morning, and he was warm and dry and could smell coffee. He found himself beneath a huge lean-to, lying under some bear skins. He was tightly bandaged. A huge man, bearded, squatted over a fire.

John Trotter said he had found him, made him stay under the lean-to for another day, and then the two of them went up into the mountains together. Trotter got him back on his feet, showed him how to trap beaver, and how to skin them.

A month later, Trotter went back with him to the ferry

to get his horse. When they left, the building was a blazing fire, the old man and one son were dead, and another son and the daughter had been cut adrift on the ferry.

The two of them returned to the mountains to get ready for the winter. Reuben stayed with him for eight years.

When the Civil War broke out, Trotter decided to go back home, saying something about being fifty and an old Virginian, and it was stupid, he knew, but he reckoned it would have to be done anyhow. He told Reuben to stay and tend the traps and he would be back.

Two years later, Cal Koller came by and passed word to Reuben that John Trotter was dead. Cal spent the night, and they sat up together with Cal smoking his pipe and telling stories about him. Koller said that Lee had come by one day and told Trotter he had heard he was a good marksman. They were under fire from a company of artillery dug in up on a bank on the other side of a creek. Lee had asked him *how* good he was; Trotter told him to call off the time, leveled his rifle and started firing, picking off one of the gunners on the other side. He reloaded and fired again, and again, as someone kept jumping up to replace the men who fell. Lee kept time; when he called a halt there were forty hit in thirty minutes.

After Cal left, Reuben brought in the traps, closed up the cabin, and got his horse. He headed down out of the mountains and went due east. He had made up his mind to go find where Trotter was buried, claim the body, maybe get it wrapped proper, and bring it back and bury it in the mountains. He told himself it was stupid, but he reckoned it would have to be done anyhow. So he went and did it.

He lived with a Shoshoni woman for a year and a half. He had come down to Abilene one time to sell some beaver, planning on staying for two, three days. He rode up one street and down another, taking his time, getting a good look at everything, in no hurry for a drink, a bath, or supper. He noticed on one street a structure that looked like a small corn crib built up against the outside wall of a harness shop. Someone was inside it.

He moved his horse across the traffic and took a closer look. It was a woman, an Indian woman, a Shoshoni. The door was locked with a chain.

He came closer and said, in Shoshoni, "Hello."

She didn't answer him; she didn't even look at him.

He said, "Sister, greetings."

She still didn't answer. He backed off and left.

Later, that afternoon, he saw the woman being led down the street. The man was tall, skinny, his face shaven but with long sideburns, his pants tucked into the top of his boots. She had a leather strap around her neck and a chain attached to the strap. He seemed greatly amused at leading her around.

Reuben ran into the sheriff savoring a late afternoon drink and mentioned the Shoshoni woman. The sheriff said he wasn't happy about it but she belonged to the man, he owned her, and he wasn't breaking any law that he knew about.

A drummer standing at the bar said, "Hell, that woman

must be at least thirty. She's probably been passed around so many times she can't keep track. Listen, I can give you the name of a man who can find you all the fifteen-year-old Kiowas, Comanches, and Cheyennes you want. You ask me, the guy's welcome to her, chain or not."

Reuben looked at him and said, "I didn't ask *you* a thing," and walked out.

Later that night, he drifted into one of the larger saloons to watch a card game for a while. About fifteen minutes later, the man came walking in with the Shoshoni woman and a couple of people bought him a drink and some things were said and people laughed. He finally worked his way over to sit in the game Reuben was watching. He had the woman sit on the floor beside him, attaching the chain to the chair.

Reuben said, "No."

He wasn't heard at first. He reached down and got the woman up. She looked at him quickly.

The man said, "What the hell are you doing?"

Reuben spoke to the woman in Shoshoni. "Sister, this is no good. I am sorry, but I must do something."

The man said, "What are you telling her?" He yanked on the chain and said, "Sit down!"

Reuben had his knife out and was lightning quick in cutting off the leather strap. He wrapped the chain twice around the man's neck, stood very close and said, "I believe this belongs to you."

No one moved. Everything stopped. The man was terrified. Reuben produced a small tote bag and stuffed it in the man's belt.

"There's a hundred dollars. The woman belongs to me. If you don't agree with the sale, tell me right now . . . I didn't think so."

They left Abilene that night. They went back up into the mountains. It was three days before he could get her to say anything to him, and that was simply to say no when he asked her finally if she wanted him to take her back to her people.

She cooked for him and he showed her the traps. He talked to her at night whether she answered him or not, and it was a month before he told her he was a patient man, but he was not a saint. He put her in his bed and she stayed there.

She only said it to him once, but that was enough for him. One day, when there was three feet of snow and he had cut some wood and was carrying it in before it got dark, he slipped and went off an icy ledge about ten feet onto his back. She was there almost as soon as he hit. When he smiled and said, "If it wasn't for you sitting on my chest, I think I'd be all right," she suddenly put her head down on his chest. There were tears in her eyes and she said softly, "Brother, I love you with all my heart."

They lived together for a year and a half. It was something he tried not to think about anymore, at least not too often. Sometime late in the fall they were coming back from the traps. She was riding ahead of him; he had dropped back about forty feet, having some trouble with a cinch strap. She came around a turn, working her way up the mountain toward the cabin, and suddenly she saw five Comanches waiting. They were utterly still, sitting their horses, two on one side of the trail and three on the other. The leader motioned for her to say nothing.

She looked at him for a moment and said, very loud, "Brother, I thank you for Abilene." Then she gave off a wild Shoshoni war cry, spurred her horse, left the path, and rode straight at the three on her left. She was shot immediately.

It saved his life. He heard her and pulled out his rifle and kicked his horse into motion and saw the Comanches as he came around the turn. He shot one with the rifle at once, pulled his revolver, shot two more and kept coming.

When it was over, four were dead and one had ridden off. He was wounded in two different places. She was dead. He picked her up, took her back to the cabin, and buried her, then sat in a corner for two days and ignored the traps. He finally got up and packed. He figured he'd leave the mountains for a while, go somewhere else, come back another time.

So he came down out of the mountains and signed on with the railroad to supply them with buffalo meat.

CHAPTER 5

Once he located a herd, it was not hard to shoot six buffalo. He had that done before ten o'clock in the morning. He left the skinners butchering the meat and loading it on the wagons. He rode a wide circle, crossing five miles below the work train, his horse stepping over the bare tracks, coming back around to where rails would be laid in a few days.

He saw some signs, but nothing important, nothing serious. The work was being done too far north for Apache, and not west enough yet to run into the Sioux or Cheyenne. He decided to go back.

It was late in the afternoon, a little colder as the sun went down. Steam pressure was still being maintained in the engine and smoke marked the clear sky. He could hear an Irish crew sing out as they swung one of the 700-pound rails off the flatcar and laid it smoothly across the ties. He couldn't imagine how anyone could work a job like that. All you needed was a horse and a gun and you could go up in the mountains and have the one thing he thought a man couldn't live without—freedom.

He took care of his horse first and then got a cup of coffee from the kitchen car and found Clayton.

"I took a look around."

"What did you find?"

"Nothing."

"You must be slipping."

Reuben sipped the coffee and said, "No, I'm not slipping."

"You didn't see any Indian signs? Jesus, Meryl Baker came in here three hours ago with half a tribe. I asked you to take a look around, you come back and say you didn't see anything, and I've got Indian signs up to my ears."

Reuben gave him a look, a steady look. "I didn't figure you wanted me to tell you everything I saw. I saw a pack of wolves waiting their chance at a baby buffalo. I saw three buzzards circling a fox with a bad leg. I didn't figure you were interested in that. I figured you only wanted to know if I saw anything you ought to worry about, and I didn't. If Meryl Baker brought any Indians in here, they must be Shoshoni, because that's all that's around here. And if he did, he can turn right around and let them go back out of here."

"I don't know one Indian from another," Clayton said. "I do know an Indian from a white man. I don't trust half the white men I see, and I don't trust *any* Indian I come across."

"I told you before, the Shoshoni are not going to bother you. In a couple of weeks you'll be crossing the land of the Cheyenne. Then you'll see Meryl Baker pull his pay and go looking for a job somewhere else."

"I'll cross that bridge when I come to it. Right now, I got Indians my scout tells me are dangerous."

Reuben finished the coffee and said, "Where's he got these Indians?"

"On the other side of the water car."

Reuben turned and started away.

Clayton yelled, "Hey, don't antagonize Baker. I don't got time to go hunting for another scout."

"What difference does it make? You got this far without one."

The Indians were penned up in the open air. A makeshift rope corral had been set up behind the water car. There were ten of them, sitting on the ground. There were three old men, four women, and three kids. They were all Shoshoni.

Reuben looked them over and then walked across the tracks toward the tents set up by the hucksters and gamblers. Meryl Baker was having a drink at a temporary bar. He wore an old Army campaign hat. He was tall, dark, arrogant. He wore Army breeches stuck in his boots and a wool shirt with a greasy vest. He was talking to a group of shanty town people. Whatever he was saying, they thought it was funny. Two women came over; neither one of them was quite ready for the night.

Reuben stopped on the edge of the group and waited. Meryl Baker saw him and snapped off his drink.

Reuben said, "I heard you ran into some hostile Indians."

"That's my job."

"What were they threatening you with, Baker? Did one of the old men shake a rattle at you?"

"Look, Cameron, I don't tell you how to shoot buffalo—don't you tell me how to scout Indians. My job is to see that the Union Pacific railroad is not impeded by *any* Indians. The way I do that is my business."

"You do know a Shoshoni when you see one, don't you?"

"I know a hell of a lot more than you think I do."

"Then you know you'd be safer sleeping out there with those Shoshoni tonight than sitting in here playing cards," Reuben said.

"That's your opinion."

"What are you going to do with them?"

"That's up to Clayton. Or Mr. Casemont."

"I suggest you let them go."

"Put it in writing. As far as I'm concerned, those Indians are on their permanent reservation right now."

Someone yelled to Reuben that the wagons were coming in with the buffalo meat. He hesitated. He looked at Meryl Baker for a moment, then changed his mind and walked away.

Someone said, "What's he got to say about what you do, Baker?"

"Nothing. Not a damn thing."

Someone else said, "You know what we ought to do? We ought to hang a couple of those Indians tonight and leave them hanging here when we leave tomorrow as an object lesson to anybody who comes by."

Baker poured himself another drink. "Yeah," he said. "Maybe we should."

Reuben took his plate of beans, buffalo meat and biscuits out away from the tracks and railroad cars and found a place to eat alone.

He had made up his mind. He would finish out the month, but then he was leaving. He had shot enough buffalo to last him a long time. Maybe he'd go back up and see if the cabin was still there. He wouldn't stay, but it would be nice to look around.

It was dark when he finished eating. Lanterns were being lit up and down the track, in most of the cars, and on the other side of the tracks in the gambling tents. The card games had started.

He cleaned his plate and cup, put them away, and took a walk to find Clayton. He had considered simply opening the corral and letting them leave the camp, but then decided he should talk to the boss first.

He found him in his car, smoking a pipe and reading some maps. He stood at a slanted board checking distances.

"Clayton, I came about those Indians."

"Christ, Reuben, don't you have anything better to do?"

"I talked to Baker. He said it's up to you or Casemont. As far as he's concerned, they can rot right where they are."

"You want to talk to Jack Casemont about it?"

"If I have to."

"Do you know how much sympathy you'd get? None. When we were at Julesburg, the hustlers and gamblers had gotten out of hand. We had some shootings, some knifings, some bad scenes. Jack didn't mind the drinking and the carrying on, but he said we couldn't afford losing good men on our track crews. So he passed out rifles. He picked the meanest rail workers we had and took them into town. They walked alongside each other, slowly, up one street and down another. When they finished, the place was quiet and somebody had a lot of gamblers to bury. He isn't going to lose any sleep over a few damn Indians."

"Clayton, those Indians aren't bothering your railroad. They aren't causing you to lose any time, and they aren't forcing you to lose good men. That's just the way Meryl Baker is. I knew him at Fort Sills. He's no damn good."

"If you two got bad blood between you, that's your business for another time. My only concern is laying track." He went back to studying the maps.

"I don't like them penned up like that."

"Reuben, let it rest a couple of days. There are two hundred men in that shanty town. Give them a chance to get used to those Indians sitting out there and they'll soon lose interest. I'll let them go then. Do something now, and there'll be hell to pay."

Shorty Sullivan climbed into the car. He wore an old derby hat and a white shirt with the sleeves rolled up. He had a toothpick in his mouth. He said, "Boss, there's a man outside looking for Cameron."

"Tell him to come in."

Henry Butler climbed up the steps and came into the car. He peered through the bright light of a huge, hanging kerosene lamp. He looked closely at the two men.

"Is that you, Reuben?"

"My God. Henry."

"You look bigger. And meaner."

"You're a long way from home."

"I feel like it." He stepped in closer.

"Where are you headed?"

"Here. I've been looking for you. Your pa needs you."

"Not my pa. He's never needed anyone a day in his life."

"He does now. He's flat on his back. He's been run off his place."

"He wouldn't go."

"Dahlman put a bullet in him. Burned down the house, took the stock."

"That was a mistake."

"I know. He don't."

He looked at Roberts and said, "Clayton?"

"Sure."

"Your man Carleton's ready. Just find a gun for him. He can hit a buffalo fifty feet away. Take him off the wagon and you'll have yourself a first-class buffalo hunter."

"No problem. You want to go, you go. I'll take care of everything."

"What about the Indians?"

"I'll talk to Mr. Casemont myself tomorrow. I'm sure something can be worked out."

Reuben hesitated.

Clayton took his arm. "Go. I'll take care of it, I promise you. I'll have a talk with Baker, too. I'll tell him to count the whole thing as experience and have him look for Cheyenne. I'll take care of the Indians. You just go."

"All right."

Reuben and Henry left the car. Clayton told Shorty, "Get me some coffee. And pour a little of that Irish whiskey in it, too."

"Do you want me to remind you tomorrow to talk to Mr. Casemont?"

"About what?"

"Those Indians."

"You crazy? I got no time to fool around with a bunch of Indians."

Reuben led Henry in the dark to where he kept his horse stabled. He talked softly to the horse, rubbed its nose, and slipped on the bridle. He got it saddled, collected his gear, loaded the Sharps, and led the horse away from the railroad car.

He said to Henry, "I've got something to do before I go." He swung up in the saddle and said, "I'll meet you over that way. There's a stand of trees there."

He crossed the tracks and came down the back side where the Indians were penned. He slipped off his horse and came over to the gate. A man stood there, holding a rifle. He looked bored.

"Did Meryl Baker leave you here?"

"Yeah. Who are you?"

"Stand over here and take a good look. Do you know me now?"

"Yeah. You're the buffalo hunter."

"That's right. So don't cause me no trouble. Now, you got the Indian ponies in here, too?"

"Yeah." He said it quickly, anxious to please. "They're over there."

"Get them and bring them here."

"All right."

Reuben went over to where the Indians were sitting on the ground. He said in Shoshoni, "Who makes the decisions?"

One of the old men said, "I do."

"Bring everyone over to the gate. Your horses will be ready. I'm turning you out."

He got them over to the gate, mounted, and said, "Go due north for a while, at least one good day. Then you can go anywhere you want."

They passed him slowly in the dark. He sat his horse and waited while they rode past him and moved off away from the train. He gave them five minutes and then said to the guard, "You can go anywhere you want. I'll go tell Baker myself."

Baker was sitting in a card game. He wasn't winning. He wore his campaign hat tilted forward and was smoking a cigar. The smoke hung heavy in the large tent. The game was one of seven being played. There was a crowd at the tables and the bar.

Reuben left the Sharps with the horse and walked back through the tent. He took his time. He put a small chew in the side of his mouth. He stepped around where Baker could see him.

"Meryl, you got a minute?"

Baker looked up over the top of his cards. "I'm busy."

"Remember Fort Sills?"

"I told you I'm busy."

"Remember the squaw? The Apache woman?"

Baker played a card and didn't look up.

Reuben said, "The one you shot? The one with the baby? The one you bet you could put a bullet through her and the baby at the same time?"

Baker finally put the cards down on the table. He wet his lips, but kept his hands still. He said, "I told you what happened."

"You were lying."

Baker sat very still. Beads of perspiration ran down from his sideburns. He said, carefully, "It wasn't the way it looked."

"She was just sitting there waiting. She had been in custody three days. She was waiting to be taken to the reservation. You took out your gun ten feet away and shot her. She didn't even know who you were."

Baker didn't look up. He barely breathed. He said, "I was drunk. I had had a fever and had been sick and was drunk. *I told you that.*"

"Baker," he took a step closer, "you didn't even hit the kid the first time. You shot him after you shot his mother out from under him."

The back of the scout's shirt was marked with sweat. He said, with great effort, "I was sorry."

Reuben backed off. He said, "I turned your Indians

loose tonight. They're gone. I wanted to tell you that before I left."

He turned and walked out, his back to Baker. He
thought at first he might have cut it a little too fine when
he suddenly turned, pulling his gun. But he saw that
Baker was on his feet, and had his gun out, and was just
bringing it up to shoot him in the back.

Reuben fired. A red mark appeared over Baker's right
eye where the bullet went in. By the time he hit the floor,
Reuben was gone.

CHAPTER 6

It was raining when they spotted Abilene. It was two o'clock in the afternoon. They had been making good time the last week. The rain came down steady, but they held the herd in a direction that would bring them straight into the loading pens. Everyone was glad to get there and get it done.

Tom Cameron was trail boss. It was the third trip he had made to Abilene. He wore a yellow slicker and rode a big brown, and was glad the rain was steady and there was no thunder or lightning. He didn't want to lose any cows at the last minute.

They got the herd into town, penned in and counted, and Tom sat inside and enjoyed a hot cup of coffee. He set up a table, paid his riders, and gave them two days off. Then he watched them leap on their horses and rear back in the rain and go racing off for some faro and whiskey and a dance-hall girl.

Harlan Davis stepped inside the small stockyard office, shaking off the rain, and said, "The Double D's in town."

Tom said, "They are?"

"Yep. I saw that damn Bunny Allen at the Alamo. He was going in when I came by. I heard they got in yesterday."

Tom smiled easily. "Hell, Harlan, think how they'll feel when someone says the Bar T's in town. Let it ruin their day. They are not going to ruin mine."

"Yeah. Well, you know as well as I do that sometime before we leave town all hell is going to bust loose."

"Not necessarily. You worry too much, Harlan. Go get a drink and find somebody's fanny to pat and I'll join you when I'm done."

"You don't need me?"

"No."

"Okay, Tom. I'll be over at the Alamo."

The stock agent came in, a short man in a town hat with his sleeves rolled up, chewing on the end of a dead cigar. He said, "I remember your first trip to Abilene. You still don't drink whiskey?"

"I still don't drink whiskey."

"I'd offer you a drink to seal the deal if you did."

"Jesus, Les, the deal was sealed when you told me you'd take my cows."

Les poured himself some whiskey in a cup, put the bottle back in a file cabinet, and sat down. "The first time you came in here I thought you were some kid. When you told me you were the trail boss, I thought it was a joke. I honestly did. I thought someone put you up to it. You don't look any older now."

"I'm twenty-seven. It's the clean living. That and prayer."

"Yeah, I've seen you pray—two years ago when you tangled with Red Hartman."

"That man did have a one track mind, didn't he?"

"He don't now."

Tom finished the coffee, stood up and stretched. "I think I'll go get something to eat."

"Tom."

"What?"

"Be careful."

Tom smiled. "You sound like my mother."

"When the Double D came in here yesterday, nothing suited them. They were miserable. They had a lot of trouble on the trail, said they lost almost five hundred cattle. That Bunny Allen complained the whole time he was in here. He was looking for someone to dump all his troubles on."

"That was yesterday. Now he's had a chance to get a drink and a decent meal and a good night's sleep, and maybe even someone to rub his back. He'll be all right."

Les lowered his voice. "The man's no good. I wouldn't trust my horse with him two minutes."

"I'll buy him a drink."

"You do that, but don't turn your back on him."

"You come over later on and I'll buy you a drink, too."

"That's what you think. Until either the Double D or the Bar T leaves town, I'm not leaving this office."

"Are those your final words, Lester?"

"That's it."

Tom smiled. "I'll bring you one back."

He was the last one to leave home. He was in no hurry to go. It wasn't even his idea at first.

His father came to him and said, "You're twenty years

old. You're the best cowboy I ever seen. You could do more with cows when you were fifteen than I could when I was thirty. You deserve more than I can give you here.

"I got a note for you. It's for a Charles Collins down in Oklahoma. He's got a big ranch. I want you to go down there for a while. He knows me. He'll take you on. It'll give you a chance to make something of yourself."

They talked about it some more, but it ended up with him leaving two days later. The night before, his mother had come in, stood half in the dark and said, "I heard what your father told you the other day. He was right: You are good working with the cows. But before you leave here, you should know that your father did things a long time ago no one else could do. He was very good, too. There was *no one* who ever worked any better than your father. You remember that."

He lay in the dark and said, "I will."

"I know we may never see you again. I want you always to respect your father."

He knew his mother was crying, and he almost decided not to go.

She said, with effort, "Your father loves you three boys. It has been killing him to see each one of you go. And yet he's so proud of each one of you. I just want you to be proud of him."

At breakfast, Tom said to his father, "I hope this place don't fall apart once I go. You've picked up a lot of bad habits lately, so I've written down some instructions." Keeping a straight face, he dug a piece of paper out of his shirt pocket. "I think I've covered everything. If you run into something you can't handle, check what I wrote down here. It'll tell you how to do it."

He stood up to go saddle his horse. He said, "Stick this up somewhere in the kitchen so you can find it when you need it. Maybe if you'd check over this list now and then, things would improve around here."

He put the paper on the table, went to the door, and said, "Ma, keep after him, will you? Don't let him lose that paper, because anyone who follows exactly what's written down on that paper can't help but know how to run a ranch. Anybody who follows what's written there will have a jump on everyone else. If I must say so myself, the person who wrote that out is just this side of being a genuine, pure genius."

He left.

His father stared at the paper.

His mother said, "You know what that is, don't you?"

"Yeah."

"That's the paper you gave him when he was ten, on his birthday. You said you wrote down a few things for him to follow. You said that if he did, he would never go wrong."

"I remember."

"He's kept it all this time."

Frank Cameron got up and with due deliberation stuck the paper onto the wall just above the sink.

It took him two weeks to reach the Bar T. Charles Collins took one look at the note he had and gave him a job.

"So you're Frank Cameron's boy."

"Yes."

"If you've got half the sense he does, you'll be running this place for me in ten years."

It wasn't dealing poker on a riverboat, or panning for gold in California, but it was what Tom wanted. He was up at four, spent his days eating dust, pulling dumb cows out of bogs, sweating in the summer and freezing in the winter. He struggled with blizzards and thunder storms, and dealt with trees to run into and holes for horses to step in. He ate what was cooked and slept with fifteen other men in the same room. When he made his first trail drive north, he had to swim muddy rivers, skirt prairie fires, and worry constantly about stampedes.

He made his first drive the second year he was there. He was positive about most things, and he never borrowed trouble. He got along easily with most people, and he never wore a gun ("I can't get into trouble if I don't have a gun"), but he could shoot. He was quick and sharp-eyed and had no trouble hitting anything he wanted to hit.

At the end of the fourth year, Charles Collins said, "I'm not going to wait ten years."

"For what?"

"To put you in charge. When the herd goes north this year, you're trail boss. I already told Doug, and he agrees. Harlan will be your second in command."

The drive went off without a hitch, and he came back and helped Collins increase his stock, seeing to it that things went the way Charles liked them to go. Charles

Collins went East that winter on the first extended vacation he had ever taken. He went without a worry in the world.

Tom left the stockyards and went downtown. There was bad blood between the Double D and the Bar T, and he knew he had a problem. To start with, Charles Collins and Matt Fillinbright couldn't stomach each other. And, Bunny Allen had killed a Bar T rider the last time they were in Abilene, which didn't set too well. He figured if everyone from the Bar T would take it easy and concentrate on having a good time, and the Double D would pull out tomorrow, things might work themselves out. At least that was the way he was going to play it.

The Alamo was the largest saloon in Abilene. It had a big room with a forty-foot front on Cedar Street and an entrance at each end. The front entrance had three double-glass doors that were always open. There was a long bar with brass fixtures and mirrors, paintings of nudes, green gaming tables, and a small orchestra that played in the morning, afternoon, and night, competing with clinking glasses, shouts, laughs, curses, and gunfire at times.

Tom went first to the hotel for supper, had a bath, a shave, and his hair trimmed, then stopped in at the Alamo to look around before going to bed. It seemed funny having few responsibilities, knowing that the men were on their own. If they wanted, they would meet the day after tomorrow and start back to Oklahoma. Until then, they could spend their money any way they pleased. The hot supper and hot bath after that cold all-day rain had made him sleepy, and he didn't figure to stay long.

The Alamo was crowded; all the gaming tables were full. There were spectators standing around watching, waiting a turn, an empty chair. There was very little room for anyone at the bar.

Cowboys were scattered in among railroaders, soldiers, miners, Texans, sheepherders wearing one spur, gamblers, and local people. There were at least fifteen women in the room earning their money pleasing, entertaining, and pushing drinks.

Tom drifted through the crowd. He liked the noise and excitement, but he didn't drink and he didn't gamble. He made friends easily, and he liked to sit in a crowded room and swap range talk, stories, and jokes.

Harlan came up to him with a drink in his hand and half a smile on his face, and said, "Tom, take a look at that redhead over there. Did you ever see a woman as pretty as that?"

"That one with her arm around that railroader?"

"No! Jesus, Tom, the girl I'm talking about would never look twice at any damn railroader. Over there, see her?"

"Yeah. The one that's bowlegged. I see what you mean, Harlan, she is kinda pretty."

"Her legs ain't bowed! You can't even see her legs from here."

Someone else yelled at Tom, and Harlan moved away, saying, "You come over later and I'll introduce you. Her name is Alice."

A big man dressed in a suit and tie, and with a watch chain across the front of his vest, stuck out his hand. "I'm John McCabe, from Dodge. Can I buy you a drink?"

"No, thanks." Tom shook his hand.

"I hear you lost only thirty head coming up from Oklahoma. That is damn good. I am in shipping, for the Tri-State Shipping Corporation. We've been in Dodge now for seven years. Our prices are as competitive as any you'll find here. Better, in fact. Let me give you my card."

"The last time anyone gave me a card, it was the eight of diamonds."

"This card will get you an immediate ten percent bump over the going rate for cattle in Abilene the first time you bring a herd into Dodge."

"Well, if I had a card, which I don't, and gave it to you, which I would if I had one, it would get you first pick of the bunks the first night you spend on the Bar T. Which is another way of saying that if you want to talk about the weather, you've got the right man, but if you want to talk business, you'll have to talk to Mr. Collins."

"Tell him what I said. Give him the card. Dodge City can make it worthwhile to bring your cows over there instead of Abilene."

"Come down and tell him yourself. It's not that far. He'd be glad for the company, and you'd enjoy the country."

John McCabe held out his hand. "I might do that, friend."

They shook hands and he left.

Ernie Lakeland came over and said, "Boss, I think you

better come over here. The kid's got a problem. Two Double D riders are trying to brace him."

"Where?"

"The monte table."

They worked their way over through the crowd to the table. A young boy, barely seventeen, was staring at two men across from him. He wore his hat hanging down his back from a string looped around his neck. The two Double D men were separated by a gambler and a small rancher. No one was moving. One of the men wore gloves. The other one wore a large Mexican sombrero.

Tom came toward the table and said to the boy, "Hey, Larry, you promised to buy me a drink. I'm ready."

The young boy tried to look over. He managed to say, "Maybe later. I think I'm busy."

"Jesus, kid, you can gamble anytime. I only take a drink once a year, and this is it. You said you would buy. Come on, let's go."

The man with the Mexican sombrero said, "He said he was busy."

"I know, but you don't understand. I actually got two drinks coming. Look, this gentleman will take his place, won't you?" He motioned to a bystander.

"I suggest you go buy yourself a drink. He ain't going nowhere."

Tom ignored the man. He said, "Larry, five minutes. I drink fast. Buy me one drink and then you can come right back."

The boy said, in a low voice, "They said something about my father."

"Maybe they know him. Come on, I want my drink."

"I can't."

Tom looked at him. Larry had been with the Bar T for three years. He had wandered in one day, alone, and had been adopted by everyone. He worked hard and never bothered anyone and very seldom said anything. Everyone liked him, and Tom knew he was going to get him out of there.

He turned with a big smile, holding his arms out wide, and faced the two men. "Hey, it's been decided. The kid and I are going to go get a drink. You can come along if you want. He's buying. Or you can stay here and play, but he and I are leaving. Together."

One of them said, "You're leaving. He ain't."

"Yes, he is."

Ernie came back through the crowd. Six other Bar T hands worked their way in toward the table. Harlan came close with a redheaded woman in tow.

Tom said, "Holy hell, *now* look. In a minute, we'll have a convention here." He put a hand on the boy's arm and said, "Let's go get us a drink."

The boy was surprised at the strength in Tom's hand. His words were spoken lightly, easily, but his fingers tightened around the kid's arm with intensity. The boy was virtually pulled out of the chair.

No one moved. The two men gritted their teeth, but they sat still. Nothing happened. Tom got the boy away from the table and over to the bar.

Tom said, "Why don't you and me turn in?"

"Now?"

"Yeah. Right now."

"It's early. This is the first time I've ever been in a place like this. I'll stay out of trouble. How about one more hour?"

"Haven't you had enough?"

"A half hour?"

"Only if you promise me to keep your head down and go to another bar. Stay in the background, and don't play cards. If anyone says anything about your father, throw in your mother and your sister, too, but don't give anyone an excuse to shoot you. It ain't worth it."

"Aw, you don't mean that."

"I sure as hell do." He turned and said, "Ernie, take the kid over to the Bull's Head. Let him look at the pictures, get a young girl to sit on his lap, but put him back in a corner somewhere, will you?"

"Sure, boss."

"All right, kid, against my better judgment, go."

"Don't worry. I'll be all right."

"Yeah, sure."

He made one more sweep around the room, shaking hands, swapping stories, and decided to call it quits. He headed for the front door.

Bunny Allen stood there. He had just come in. He was tall and slender, and wore a hat with a flat crown. He was clean shaven and dressed meticulously. He said, "I hear you've been nursemaiding again."

"Where do you buy those shirts?"

"Do you wipe his nose for him, too?"

"You look like you could use a drink. Come on, I'll buy you one."

"I could use you to mind your own business."

"I do, Bunny. You just don't give me any credit."

"And when the hell are you going to start wearing a gun?"

"You sound like you didn't have supper yet. Why don't we go over to the hotel and I'll buy you a steak? It'll put you in a better frame of mind. I had a cousin . . ."

"Don't worry about my frame of mind."

"You *are* touchy tonight. Just one thing doesn't go right and you're down on the whole world. What you need is . . ."

"Cut it out, Cameron. I've had enough of your damn humor. I don't know how in the hell you ever get one cow from the fence to the gate. You know what you look like to me? A big joke, that's what."

The front of the room got quiet. No one twenty feet around them moved. They all looked at Tom.

Bunny said, shifting his weight, "I think you're a joke, I think the Bar T is run by a joke, and I think that's all you hire because everywhere I look all I see are Bar T jokes."

Tom said, "Do you feel better now? You got all that out of your system? That's almost as good as going to church, isn't it? I'm going over to the hotel. If you want a good steak, come over. I might still be buying if you don't wait too long."

And he walked out the door.

CHAPTER 7

When he got to the hotel, an old man was sitting in the lobby, half asleep. He jumped when Tom came in.

Henry Butler said, "Tom. Tom Cameron."

"Lord, look what's come up out of the ground."

They shook hands.

Tom said, "Where did you come from?" He looked around.

"I'm alone. You weren't looking for your pa, were you?"

"A little."

"That's why I'm here. He needs you."

"Did he forget which side you brand the calves on?"

"He got burned out. And shot. I got him holed up in a dugout with a half-breed woman. He can't get around too well, but he should be all right if no one finds him there. He didn't tell me to come, but I figure if he don't get some help, he ain't going to make it."

"Come on, I'll buy you supper. We'll leave in the morning."

Tom got ahold of Harlan and turned everything over to him. He gave him a note to take back to Charles Collins and then went to bed. He figured they'd get a few hours' sleep and be on their way before it was light.

An hour after he went to sleep, he was awakened. It was Harlan, and he looked sick. He sat back on a chair and waited until Tom sat up on the side of the bed.

"It's the kid. He's dead."

Tom just looked at him.

"It was Bunny Allen. He found the kid in the Bull's Head and started to bait him. Ernie got word to me and I went right over, but it was done when I got there."

"It was just Bunny?"

"Yeah. That was enough. But, Tom . . ."

"What?"

"He shot him five times. He shot him four times after he was already down."

Tom stood up and started to dress. He said, "Where is he?"

"The kid?"

"Yeah."

"We got him down near the pens. We wrapped him up and put him in one of the wagons."

"Tell somebody to stay with him."

"Okay."

Tom went out the door and started down the hall.

Harlan said, "Tom."

He stopped.

"The kid did pretty good, just like you told him. Bunny started in and got nowhere. Then he said something about the kid's father and mother, but the kid just kept quiet. He was watching a faro game and never let on like he heard anything."

"What happened?"

"Bunny said something about you."

"Me?"

"He said you were yellow and the kid hit him. With his fist. Knocked him flat on his back. He never went for his gun. Bunny shot him from the floor, while the kid was waiting for him to get up."

The Bar T riders were waiting in the street near the Bull's Head. They were in an ugly mood.

Tom said, "Ernie, can I borrow your Winchester?"

"Sure, boss. I'll go get it."

Tom said, "What's it like in there, Curley?"

The oldest man in the group spat a stream of tobacco juice and said, "Kinda quiet. They're thinking it over. I think they know now they bit off more than they can chew."

"Where's Bunny?"

"At the faro table, the one sitting in the center of the room."

Ernie came up and handed the rifle to Tom. "It's ready."

"All right, I'll be right out."

"What about us?"

"Wait here. I don't want to make the man nervous."

Curley said, "He's got help to his right, and one to his left, back near the wall near the poker table. And there's one at the end of the bar."

"He'll need it," Tom said, and started toward the door.

Then he stopped and said, "Listen. If I don't come out and he does, kill him for me."

There was still a crowd inside. The gambling and drinking continued, but almost in slow motion, as if everyone was just killing time. They knew something was going to happen.

Tom went past the bar, the rifle in one hand, pointing at the floor. When he came into the room where the gaming tables were, the talk stopped. Bunny Allen sat right in front of him at the center table, a cigarette in his mouth. He sat hunched forward, both elbows on the table, looking at his cards. When Tom walked in, the other players got up and left the table. Bunny sat back.

"I see you got yourself a gun." He took a deep drag on the cigarette. "Is that the best you can do?"

Tom held the rifle straight down at his side. He smiled a little and said, "You should have come over to the hotel and had that steak. You made the wrong decision."

"That's what you think."

"I should have killed you two years ago."

"You couldn't do it then and you can't do it now."

"I am about to put that cigarette out."

Bunny pulled his gun, coming away from the table in a crouch. Tom raised the rifle to his hip, fired, and killed him instantly. He turned and shot the man to the left, then swung back and hit the man on the right. Just as quickly he snapped off a shot that took down the man at the bar. He hadn't once put the rifle to his shoulder.

He was nicked in the upper left arm and once across the top of his shoulder. Bystanders afterward would say that he had gotten off some lucky shots. He didn't care what they said. He didn't plan on coming back and doing it again.

Henry Butler felt a little better when he heard what had happened. He had been having second thoughts since he tracked down Reuben Cameron. Jim Dahlman had close to a hundred men working for him, and could get another hundred if he wanted to. Henry thought maybe he should have left the boys alone. All he had been thinking about was Frank, with his leg shot up and stuck in a hole in the ground with a half-breed woman. When he stuck his head out again, Dahlman would have somebody blow it off. At the time, all Henry could think about was to go get some help, and the only help he could think of was Frank's three boys. But now he wasn't sure, because somebody was going to get hurt before it was all said and done.

He decided to go to St. Louis and look up an older sister. He wasn't moving as well as he did ten years ago and thought he'd just be in the way if he went back with Tom, so he decided to go to St. Louis for a while. Maybe he'd come back later and see how Frank was doing.

CHAPTER 8

Each morning the first thing he did was test the leg. Even before he opened his eyes, he'd move it a little, check the amount of pain, compare it against the day before, see how easy it would move, and how far.

It had been four days since Henry had carried him in from the wagon, and Frank Cameron noticed some improvement. The bullet had not touched the bone, and it hadn't torn an artery. It had ripped the hell out of the muscle, but that would heal. He could get that back in time.

He swung himself out of bed, then he sat back down. Damn, that hurt. He looked around the room. It was empty. He put his hat on and decided to give it another try. He pushed himself up on his feet, gritted his teeth and held on, and stayed up this time. He waited a long minute until things settled down, planning on trying for the table, when the woman came in.

She was carrying some water. He hadn't gotten a good look at her yet. The first two days he had slept a lot, the room was usually dark, and she never came near him any more than necessary. The young girl would usually bring him something to eat.

She walked over to the fireplace as though he wasn't standing there. He decided to give it a shot. He pushed off and managed to reach the table, favoring the leg, and wishing he had stayed where he was. He sat down on the chair. She got him something to eat and went back to the fireplace. She didn't talk to him.

He studied her. She was pushing forty, he thought, but she didn't look too bad. He couldn't tell that much from her dress. She wore, he guessed, whatever she could get, but she didn't dress like a squaw. He shifted his weight and touched his leg gingerly. She was not his problem.

The young girl was about seventeen. She spoke to him a little if he said something, but not much. She and the woman would sit together at night with the lamp turned down low, and talk in low tones as he slipped in and out of sleep. He guessed they were not related, but he didn't know much more than that. They took good care of him; he did know that much. They seemed somehow to watch him and know when he wanted something, and he would get it. So he was satisfied, at least for the first week. All he thought about up to then was his leg. He deliberately chose not to think about the ranch, or if Dahlman might come back looking for him.

One day during the second week, he spent the afternoon at the table leafing through an old catalog. Half the pages were missing; he was bored. The woman and girl were not there. He passed the time keeping the fire in the rough-stone fireplace going, keeping the chill off the room. It had been roofed with poles and covered with grass and earth, and the air was usually damp and cold. The fire provided light and warmth.

He tried to keep a good bed of hot ashes under the fire. Moving to the wood pile in the corner, he noticed something up on the wall, in the corner where the woman slept. He limped over. It was a piece of mirror, broken out of a larger one, the edges jagged, a crack down the center.

He looked in it and stood very still. He couldn't believe it. He was pale, sick looking, dirty, and disgusting. Christ, he thought, someone should just take a gun and put me out of my misery.

He worked his way out the door. It was getting late. The sun had already gone down. He stood and stared at the sunset. He hadn't done that for a long time. There was a sweet smell in the air, and he moved out of the dugout. He saw the woman around back collecting wood. She had a piece of cloth tied around her head.

He walked around to where she was. The leg hurt, but he managed pretty good as long as he took his time. He said, "Do you have a razor?"

"Yes." It surprised him hearing her talk. She didn't stop working.

"Would you get it for me?"

She straightened up. He noticed how strong she seemed.

He said, "You got any soap?"

"Yes." She stood close, but she didn't look at him.

"Get that, too. I'm going to take a bath."

"Good." It was not said loud.

"What?"

She gave him one quick look. "I said, good. You stink." And she walked off.

It had been just a quick look, but she didn't appear as old as he had thought she was; no more than forty— probably not even that.

She came back with a razor, a cake of brown soap, and a bucket of water. "This is hot, for shaving. I'll get more if you want it."

He took it over to the stream that ran close to the dugout. He took off his shirt and peeled off his undershirt. He was soft, flabby. He had no muscle tone. He looked back, embarrassed to have anyone see him. He had really let himself go.

He soaped up and shaved by touch. The razor was old but sharp. He cleaned off his face and then looked around again. He took off his boots and socks and pants, and looked at his leg. The wound had healed pretty good but there was no strength there. He waded into the water and soaped up. It was cold and he felt chilled. He decided not to take all day.

He looked up. The woman stood on the bank. "Hey," he yelled. She picked up his clothes, left clean ones, ignored him, and walked away. Damn woman, she must have been watching him get in the water. He didn't watch *her* taking a bath.

He came out, dried off, got dressed, and went back inside. He felt weak. He sat on the chair at the table. The woman worked with her back to him. He watched her for a minute.

He said, "What's your name?"

There was no answer.

"I've been here two weeks and I don't know your name."

She put a cup of coffee on the table without looking at him and went back to the fireplace.

"You speak English, I know you do. You told me I stink. What do you want me to call you?"

The young girl walked in and Frank said, "Come here. What is her name?"

She just looked at him, not sure what he wanted.

He said, "Do you know my name?"

"Yes."

"What is it?"

"Mr. Cameron."

"Okay, you know my name. I should know yours."

"Mine?"

"First yours. What is it?"

"Mary."

He spoke across the room to the woman working on supper. "See how easy that was. We now got Frank and Mary. There are three of us in this room, and we now got two names. All we need is one more and I can die happy."

She didn't look up.

He said to the young girl, "What the hell is her name? Is it something she's ashamed of? Is it Milford? Or Harry?"

"It's Tia." It was the woman. She was standing up now and looking straight at him.

"Tia?"

"Yes."

"That's better than Harry." He shook his head. "Tia is definitely better than Harry." He looked at the young girl. "She isn't your mother, is she?"

"No. My mother is dead." She went outside.

He stared at the floor and finally said, softly, "Tia, I think I should have kept my mouth shut."

Three more days went by. He had shaven and cleaned up and changed clothes, but it didn't go any further than that. The leg wasn't that much better. He walked around the room and went outside a few steps, but came right back in and rested. He didn't push it. It went slow, and he did as little as possible.

It happened in the morning. He was standing near the table when the woman came in quickly and said, "Get back in the bed. Don't move."

"What?"

"Hurry." She put her arm around his waist and moved him over into the corner. She got him down, leaned very close, and said, "Say nothing" before she left.

The girl ran in and came over to sit on the floor beside him. She said, in a desperate whisper, "Someone's coming. Don't move."

Then he heard the horse. He heard it work its way down off the slope and come in across the stream and stop. The woman was chopping wood; he heard her stop, too.

"Hey. Come here, woman." He was right outside. Frank heard him getting down. "You see any cows around here? Any Circle C cows? Did you see any of them come down here looking for water?"

She answered him in Kiowa.

"I can't understand that. English, speak English."

She said something again in Kiowa.

"I want it in English."

Again she spoke in Kiowa.

His voice was slow and hard. "Now, you speak English or I will shoot you right between the goddamn eyes."

Frank pulled his gun. He tried to get up. The young girl held him back. She shook her head no.

"What am I wasting my time with you for? The hell with it." Frank heard a crack and knew she had been hit. The cowboy said, "You stupid half-breed, I should just shoot you and do everyone around here a big favor."

Frank pushed to get up; he was furious. The girl threw herself across him and held him down. He couldn't move. He didn't have the strength to push her off. She lay on top of him, her mouth near his ear, and said, "Don't move. If he tries to come in here, she'll kill him."

He heard him get on his horse and leave. As he went back across the stream, the girl let go and sat up. She looked to see if he was all right and then went out.

He got up on his feet and went outside to join her. He looked around. They were gone, both of them. He could see the cowboy close to a mile away, but the woman and girl were out of sight. He waited awhile and then went back inside. He worked up the fire, put on some coffee, sat in the chair, and did some thinking. He was left alone all day.

The girl came back first, at supper time, and then finally the woman came in. She got some dinner, sat in the corner, and ate without a word. He left her alone.

Later that night, after they were in bed, he got up and crossed the room. He got down close to her. There was a little light from the fireplace. She lay with her face to the wall.

"Tia," he spoke softly, "tomorrow I am going to go."

She didn't move. He knew she had heard him.

"My leg is all right. I will go after breakfast."

He reached over and touched her face gently, then turned it and looked to see if she had been hurt. When he was satisfied, he said, "Thank you."

He got up and she said, "You must stay."

"No. It's too dangerous."

"You must stay. One more week."

"No."

"That other man, Henry, *su amigo*."

"Yeah?"

"He went to get your sons."

Frank stood absolutely still.

"You must wait here until they come. I promised that I would keep you alive till then. I can't do that if you leave here. When they come, then you go."

When the woman came back with some wood in the morning, he was up and dressed and shaved.

He said, "I need a horse."

She didn't move.

"I'm not leaving, but I need to start riding. A little at

least, to start with. And I need a gun. Also, from now on I get the wood."

She looked at him for a long moment, then said, "Wait here."

She dropped the wood and crossed the stream, holding her skirt up, and he was surprised at how quick she moved and how strong she seemed. She went into a ravine on the other side and dropped out of sight.

She was gone for more than fifteen minutes. Suddenly she appeared leading a horse, a large bay. It had a bridle but no saddle. She tied it fast and said, "Around here." She led him back of the dugout, up on a slight hill. She moved some bushes and he saw several hiding places, one with a deep trench in which she uncovered his saddle and war bag.

He picked up the saddle and started back. She carried the war bag. It just about played him out, and he had to wait a minute before he could put the blanket on the horse and swing the saddle up. He stuck with it, however, and got it done. He put his foot in the stirrup, took a deep breath, and swung himself up.

He looked at her and said, "I think I'll stay here now that I'm up because I don't think I can do that again."

She put her hand on his leg and said, "Don't go too far."

"I was planning on trying to make it from here to that little tree and back. If the wind's with me."

He started off slowly, and she watched as he moved across open ground and then she went inside. He was gone for a half hour. When he came in, he was pale. He

sat at the table and she fed him, and then he went to bed.
That afternoon, he got up, dug into his war bag, and
came up with his gun. He buckled it on, went out back,
and practiced drawing and shooting for an hour.

He repeated the routine the next day, and cut some
wood. He did it all again the day after, increasing the
time he spent little by little. On the fourth day Doc
Kruger appeared at the door.

"I want to see your leg. Drop your pants."

Frank looked around. The woman and girl were both in
the room.

Doc Kruger said, "They have both seen you with your
pants down. They've been nursing you for three weeks.
Come on."

The girl went outside. The woman turned her back and
worked near the fireplace. Frank opened his belt and
pulled down his pants.

Doc Kruger took a good look at his leg and said, "All
right, pull them up. That's not bad. I think you'll live."

The woman put two cups of coffee on the table and
left. Kruger sat down, took out a pipe and tamped some
tobacco into it.

Frank sat down and said, "What's Dahlman doing? He
hasn't considered going into the ministry, has he?"

"He's doing whatever he wants to do, as usual."

"Does he know I'm here?"

"I don't think so. I don't think he cares where you are.
You don't worry him. You were one of his easy problems
to solve."

"Doc, I want to ask you a question. Who is this woman? The one I'm staying with?"

"Her father was one of the first traders in the territory, forty years ago. He bought a Kiowa squaw for two necklaces. He ran a trading post for a while, did some scouting for the Army, and was killed over in New Mexico when the girl was fifteen. Her mother was killed two years later. She attached herself to a soldier, but he couldn't take the harassment with her being a half-breed, so he put her out. She married a dirt farmer in Kansas, lived with him until he was shot about five years ago, then she decided to go back home. She got this far and stayed for some reason. She never says why.

"I got the Turner brothers to help dig this place out for her. She took the girl in two years ago—her family was heading for California from Ohio with two other wagons. It's said they were hit by Comanches the other side of Ford's spring; she says it wasn't Indians. I think it was Comancheros. She wandered in here on foot and the woman took her in."

"Do you help them out?"

"No. They help me out. That woman can take care of herself."

"Do you know where Henry went?"

"I think so."

"He told you?"

Doc Kruger pointed his pipe. "He told you."

"Maybe he did, Doc, but I was in no condition to remember anything that happened that night. When he dropped me off here, he could have told me he was turning Catholic, and I wouldn't have cared."

"He said you needed help, so he was going after your boys."

"What do you think his chances are of finding them?"

"I don't know."

"I think he's got two chances, slim and none. If one of them did come back here, what would Dahlman do?"

He stood up. He knocked the ashes out of his pipe. He said, "You don't need me to tell you that."

The next day, Frank saddled the horse early and left. He was gone almost all day. When he came back, it was getting dark. The woman was sitting outside waiting for him.

He swung down off the horse slowly. He looked exhausted. The woman came over and started to loosen the cinch.

He said, "I'll do that."

She kept working.

"I'll do it. I am not a baby. I can take care of my own horse."

She looked at him. "You went too far."

"That's my business."

"As long as you're here, it's mine."

"I don't have much time. Right now I couldn't hit the ground if I threw my hat."

"You must build up your strength. You must be patient. It can't be hurried."

"It can be pushed."

"No, it can't."

"You don't understand. I have very little time. I don't have the chance to do it right. I have to do it anyway I can."

"You'll hurt yourself this way."

"No, I won't."

"Look at you. You can barely stand. It's not right to do it this way."

"There's nothing wrong with the way I'm doing this."

She gave him a hard look. "You are being stupid."

"First you tell me I stink. Now you tell me I'm stupid. You are really building up my confidence."

"These things take time."

"I don't have time. Let go of the saddle."

She held on, determined. He suddenly leaned down and kissed her. She jumped back. He swung the saddle off and said, "When you don't have strength, sometimes you have to be sneaky."

She glared at him. Then she relaxed, touched her mouth, gave him a half smile, and said, "I want to be around when you try that particular trick on Mr. Dahlman." Then she turned and walked away.

—

CHAPTER 9

It was 9 P.M. when Morgan Cameron rode into Calendar. It was Saturday night and the town was noisy. He rode down the main street and stopped at the livery stable. A young boy sat inside. A lantern was hanging on a nail.

Morgan got down and said, "Would you rub him down and feed him? Let him rest a little? I'm not staying all night."

The boy loosened the cinch and Morgan said, "Where's the best place in town to eat supper?"

"At Miller's. It's up the street beside the telegrapher's office." He ran his hand over the horse. It was a beautiful animal.

"Thanks." He handed the boy a dollar. "I'll be back." He took off his coat and left it with the horse.

He ate supper and walked out front and stood there a moment. He pulled the Bull Durham sack out of his vest pocket, rolled a cigarette and lit it, and smoked a minute, taking his time. It had been a long day and he felt a little tired. He'd get his second wind in a minute.

He looked across the street at the largest saloon in town. It was brightly lighted and noisy. He figured he might as well start there.

He flipped the cigarette away and crossed the street, going up the steps and in through the door. He stopped at the bar and got a drink. He sipped it slowly, sizing up the room. It was big and busy, but it lacked refinements. The bar was full. The bartender was fat and bald and fairly quick, and took only a passing look at Morgan. He wasn't the only one passing through. The gaming tables were busy. There were five women working the room.

Morgan carried his drink and circulated through the room. He took his time. He watched for a while and then picked the table he wanted. He waited until there was a seat available and sat down.

They were playing stud. The dealer was about thirty, good looking, with a pencil thin mustache. He was all right, but he would be in over his head at either Abilene or Dodge. There were three cowboys at the table and an older man from town. Morgan sat down and got some chips, and the cards were dealt.

He paced himself for an hour, getting the rhythm of the room, listening to the conversation that flowed back and forth. He held himself back, staying no more than ten dollars ahead, not enough to draw attention or cause any aggravation.

Finally, he decided there was no sense putting it off any longer. Between hands, while the cards were being shuffled and drinks were being brought to the table, he faced one of the cowboys. He was probably twenty-five, with bright red hair, wearing leather cuffs—an impulsive player, quick tempered, losing close to twenty dollars and becoming more aggravated with each pot he lost.

Morgan said to him, in a smooth, easy tone, "What's the biggest spread around here? I saw a lot of cows coming in."

"You don't know?" There was a touch of irritation and belligerence in his voice.

"No, I don't know."

"The Circle C."

He had drawn blood. He said, "How big is it?"

"When you leave town, you're on Circle C land. It don't matter which way you go. And if you see a cow, that's ours."

The cards were dealt, and he picked up his hand. The man from town said in a friendly tone, "He's prejudiced. Red works for the Circle C. What is it now, six years? We got three big ranches around here. This is good cow country."

"Edgar, I said the Circle C. He asked for the biggest damn spread and I told him. Holy hell, you're not including the Rocking Chair W, are you?"

"Okay, okay, don't get yourself in an uproar. The Circle C is probably the biggest. I'm not going to argue that. But the Slash J and the Rocking Chair W ain't exactly small."

"Well, they ain't exactly big, either. Christ, you could put both of them together and they wouldn't come up to us."

The man from town shrugged and made a bet.

The cowboy beside Red said, "You looking for a job?"

Morgan said, "No. I got one."

Red looked at him, his face flushed a little, and said, "Yeah? Where?"

"The Box C."

"Where the hell's that?"

"I was told when I left Calendar to head east. It straddles Crystal Creek."

The table got still. Red stared at him. He said, "There ain't no Box C."

"You sure?"

"I said so, didn't I?"

"Then I rode a long way for nothing." He kept his tone smooth, even.

"Who the hell are you?"

"Are you usually in a good mood like this?" Morgan smiled slightly.

"It's none of your business what kind of a mood I'm in."

"I guess if I played cards the way you do, I wouldn't be happy either. You've raised this hand twice already, and all you're holding is a little pair of threes."

Red's face was livid. Everyone at the table sat absolutely still. Part of the room got quiet. Some people looked over. Three or four cowboys got up in different parts of the room and drifted over.

Red said, "How would you know what I got in my hand?"

An older man, big, muscular, stepped close to the table. He said, "What's going on, Red?"

Red kept his eyes on Morgan. His hands were

clenched. He fought to control his temper. He said, with effort, "Nothing."

"Red?" The man was obviously someone in charge.

Red said, "The man said I had a pair of threes in my hand."

"So?"

"I got a pair of threes in my hand."

The dealer sat very still. A bead of perspiration appeared on his upper lip.

The older man took a good look at Morgan. He said, "Who are you, friend?"

Red said, "He said he came into town with a job promised. With the Box C."

"There ain't no Box C around here."

"That's what I told him."

The man looked at Morgan. "You winning?"

"A little."

"I think you better take what you got and call it a day."

Red said, "Floyd, let me have him. I can take him."

"I don't know."

"Floyd, I can."

The man looked at Morgan. "Can he take you?"

Morgan shook his head, slightly. "No."

A cowboy behind Morgan pulled his gun and said, "I think he can." There were now more Circle C cowboys scattered around the table, edging in closer.

Floyd said, "Maybe I should let him try now."

"It wouldn't help."

"I think it would."

The voice came from the bar. It said, "The game's over." It wasn't loud but it carried across the room.

A big man stood at the corner of the bar, looking into the room. He was bearded, with a chew of tobacco in the side of his mouth. He was holding a Sharps buffalo rifle in his arms, aimed directly at Floyd. Reuben Cameron said, "That man is going to buy me a drink. You don't mind if he leaves the table, do you?"

Floyd looked at him and the rifle. He said, "Stay out of this."

Reuben said, "I'm not as patient as he is. Raise your voice once more and I am going to pull this trigger. I don't like you. I don't like the way you look, and I don't like the way you sound. So don't aggravate me."

Floyd motioned and the cowboy behind Morgan put his gun away. Morgan collected his money and stood up.

Floyd looked at Morgan and said, "Like I said, there ain't no Box C around here, so I suggest you keep going."

"Explain that to him." He pointed to Reuben.

Floyd didn't say anything. He didn't look back at Reuben.

Morgan looked at Red. "Remember, when you've got a pair of threes, you've got nothing."

Reuben said, "What were you doing back there?"

They walked over to the livery stable and got their horses ready.

"Sizing things up."

"Did you find what you were looking for?"

"Yeah."

"What would you have done if I hadn't gotten thirsty and stopped in there for a drink?"

"Taken a job with the Circle C?"

"Morgan, I'll do you a favor. I won't mention this to Pa when we see him. He always thought you were the one with the brains."

They decided to camp north in some timber country for the night and locate the dugout in the morning.

Floyd Walker left town right after they did. He returned to the ranch. He wasn't sure what was going on, but he figured he better say something to Dahlman. He had been foreman for the Circle C for eight years and usually handled most things on his own. He was almost a carbon copy of Dahlman: He had the same drive, the same ruthlessness, the same quick grasp of situations, the same determination. He simply did not own 12,000 head of cattle.

This business tonight was strange, though, and he figured he better say something to Dahlman. It didn't add up.

It was late when he reached the ranch, but there was a light on in the house. It was a big, rectangular building, with a low porch roof but no porch. Two of the outside walls were stone, with rough timber for the other two. Dahlman had been married when he first came up from Texas, but his wife had died and he had never married again.

He sat at a desk working on some papers when Floyd

came in. He had a glass of whiskey sitting on the desk. Only one lamp was lit in the big room.

Dahlman told Floyd to pour himself a drink and sit down. "What's on your mind?"

"There was a man in town tonight playing cards. He and Red got in an argument. It was the damnedest thing. He said he had come to town because he had been promised a job with the Box C."

"The Box C?"

"Crystal Creek. Frank Cameron."

"Yeah, I remember. I shot that old bastard in the leg, didn't I? He's not still around, is he?"

"I don't know. I don't think so. No one's seen him."

"Maybe he was promised this job before we burned them out?"

"Could be."

"Who would want to work for the Box C? A place run by an old rummy like that."

"I don't think he drinks. He just looked like it."

"He looked like he should. Are you sure this guy said the Box C?"

"Yeah."

"Maybe he was mixed up."

"He didn't look like he usually got mixed up."

"Did you get his name?"

"No."

"What did he look like?"

"Thirty. Average size. He didn't dress like he worked on any ranch. I'll tell you what he looked like."

"What?"

"The way he acted, the way he handled himself, the way he set Red up, I got the feeling he was a gunfighter. We had ten of us all around him, and he just sat there like he was at home."

"You think someone's bringing him in?"

"I don't know."

"The Slash J? You think they might be bringing him in? So far we haven't had any trouble with them, but I never did trust that damn Colbert."

"I don't know. Why would he mention the Box C?"

"Colbert could have put him up to it. He couldn't have anything to do with Cameron. Jesus, Cameron couldn't bring in a preacher. Where would he find a gunfighter? What would he offer him?"

"I'm probably wrong. It was just a feeling I got. Maybe he said it just to rile Red. Maybe he *is* just passing through."

"What did you do with him?"

"Nothing. I was going to let Red have him, but some trapper pointed one of those damn buffalo guns at me and suggested we let the man go."

"Were they together?"

"Not that I could tell. This guy was standing at the bar and I think he just stuck his nose in."

"Are they still in town?"

"No. They left. They're probably halfway to Waco by now. It just seemed funny, that's all."

Dahlman sipped a little whiskey. "Let's make sure. Get Al Bluebox. Get him out of bed—tell that damn Indian to take a good look around. I want him to pick up their trail.

Find out where they are. I don't care about the trapper, but tell him to find the card player."

"All right."

"And tell him to put a bullet in his back."

CHAPTER 10

Late Sunday morning, Tom Cameron reached Circle C country. He started across the open range. It was clear and pleasant, and the sun made the day seem lazy.

Tom kept up off the flat ground, working his way along the ridges. He whistled a low tune.

He spotted a line rider late in the morning and worked his way over toward him. He looked like a drifter, without a worry in the world. He had his hat pushed low to shade his face, with a broomweed stalk stuck in the side of his mouth. His gun was rolled up in his bedroll. The bedroll was wrapped in his yellow slicker and tied behind his saddle.

The two got closer, working their horses easily, not pushing it; finally they met, pulled up, and both got down. They nodded, loosened their cinches, and hunkered down to talk a little.

"Nice day."

"It sure is." The line rider was young, pleasant, wearing a gun with the hammer tied down in the holster.

They exchanged information about the weather, calf crops, cattle prices, grass, water, horses, good card games, bad women, and available young girls on any of the neighboring ranches or with any of the nester families.

Tom said, "You been with this outfit long?"

"A year now. I was up in Montana before. Might go back there again. Or maybe into Wyoming."

"You got cows spread out over fifteen, twenty miles, it seems."

"I know. I feel like I've chased them halfway to hell."

"Did you just add to your herd?"

"I don't know. The last big decision I was in on was whether we were going to have beans again for Christmas."

"I saw some Box C cows coming over this way. Some had the brand reworked and some didn't," Tom said.

The rider looked around a little, drew some x's in the dirt, loosened his neckerchief. He said, "Did you ever work for a big spread? I can't keep track of what we have and what we don't. I don't even know if I've been over the whole ranch yet or not.

"I've been up here for a month now, and new cows show up all the time. We keep buying people out. This is not good country for small ranchers. Mr. Dahlman is determined to own everything he can see, and I'm told to just run any new cows in with the rest. We'll wait until spring to sort them out. This is what they call big business. I don't think twice anymore about seeing a strange cow. There ain't many that come in here that ever go out again."

Tom stood up. "You mean, until now."

Frank Cameron poured a cup of coffee for himself. The woman was outside. He wasn't happy with his progress, but he wasn't unhappy, either. He had pushed himself hard that morning, and it had gone half decently. He had also lost some weight and had gotten back some of his strength. He wasn't as quick as he liked to be, but it was coming around. Now if he didn't go out and get shot in the other leg, he'd be all right.

The woman came in. She stood at the door and said, "There's two men coming."

He put the cup down and got the rifle from the corner of the room.

She said, "Let me see." She went back out.

He stayed inside the door. He didn't back into the corner and hide. He was not going to let anyone hit her again.

Two horses crossed the creek, blowing hard. They stopped in front of the dugout. He was ready. He figured it was just a matter of time before someone stumbled onto him.

Then he heard a laconic voice say to the woman, "You wouldn't happen to have an old coot holed up in there, would you?"

Another voice said, "We don't blame you for hiding him when company comes. We used to do that ourselves."

He didn't step outside right away. He couldn't believe it. He knew one of them might show up sometime, and he thought he was ready for it. But it got to him for a minute, and he blew his nose. Finally, he went through the door and took a look.

Reuben and Morgan sat there, waiting.

Reuben said, "Morgan, does that look familiar to you?"

"Let's see if it can talk."

Frank Cameron looked at his two sons, shook his head and said, "If you two are old enough, come on in and I'll offer you a cup of coffee."

Tom Cameron crossed Crystal Creek up high and came down behind the dugout. If Henry had been right, this was the place.

There was smoke coming out of a chimney stuck up over the dirt bank. He walked his horse down through the trees. Then he saw the girl. She was on foot, two hundred yards from the dugout, watching him. Her legs were bare and she wore moccasins, but she was white, he was sure of that.

He waved and walked the horse over toward her. She tried to avoid him, but he was too quick for her.

"Howdy. Nice day."

She didn't answer. She watched him, intently.

"Do you live there?" He pointed to the dugout.

"Yes."

"Is your pa home?"

"I live alone."

"Are you sure?"

"Yes."

"You got yourself a nice place there. Are you prospecting or ranching?"

She just looked at him.

He thought, she's actually pretty. If you could get some decent clothes on her, she would be all right. He took his

hat off for a breather, looked around and put it back on.
"You got any spring water?"

"No."

"Coffee?"

"No."

He smiled. "What do you drink?"

"Nothing."

"And I don't suppose you eat anything, either?"

"No."

"And I should just keep going?"

"Yes."

He winked at her and started down toward the dugout.
She broke into a run, went around him, raced to the front
and ducked inside the door. A woman came out at once
and watched him.

Jesus, he thought, they're like cats, and I must be getting close to the kitten. He rode around front and saw the
two horses standing there. The woman watched him
closely.

He said to her, "Am I the last one to get here?"

Morgan stepped out of the door with a gun in his hand.
He shook his head and smiled at Tom. "I thought at least
you would be smart enough not to come back."

Tom swung down and said, "I wanted to see for myself
how you were going to handle this."

The woman did biscuits and a pie, and put beans, beef,
and potatoes on the table. They ate their fill and sat back,
rolling cigarettes or sipping coffee. They were surprised
to find their father looking as good as he did. He still

limped a little and was still washed out a bit, but he wasn't crippled or weak or hiding in a hole in the ground afraid to make a move.

Frank said, "Well, Henry got all of you here, but I don't know why. As you can see, I'm not ready to be buried yet. So you might as well go back."

Morgan said, "Is it okay if we wait until tomorrow?"

Reuben said, "I thought I'd take a look around while I'm here. See what I missed when I was a kid."

Tom said, "I haven't even been to town yet. I know it isn't Abilene or Dodge, but I would like to take a look at it again. I remember when I was nine years old, Morgan took me into the blacksmith's and there was this old man who could spit tobacco juice in two different directions at the same time. God, that was something to see when you're nine years old. I tried it myself when I got home and hit myself in the eye. Is he still around?"

Morgan said, "We'll go take a look."

Frank said, "All right, all right. I'm not deaf and I'm not dumb. If your minds are made up, let's see where we stand. Dahlman ran me clear off the Box C. He's got it now, and he's running cows on our land. He shot me in the leg, burned down my home, pulled down my fence, and he don't care if I like it or not. He's got at least ten thousand cows. His place now runs about sixty miles in any direction. He's got seventy-five, eighty men working for him, and at least twenty-five or thirty of those are hard cases. They come and go, but he's always got enough of them around. What do we have? Just the four of us."

Reuben said, "Hell, he don't stand a chance."

Morgan said, "Not the way I look at it. I feel sorry for him."

Tom said, "I think we should go get the place back. Then, if you want to leave, leave. But it should be your idea, not his."

Frank said, "How do you three figure on doing that?"

Tom said, "This is the part I'm going to like. Morgan?"

Morgan said, quietly, "I can do it."

Tom said, "I know it. I just don't know how. That's what I want to see."

Reuben said, "I figure the first thing we should do is get Pa out of here."

Frank looked across at the woman. She didn't look up. The girl was back in the corner, sitting and waiting.

Morgan said, "I agree with Reuben. You don't have to hide now."

Tom said, "If we're going to stay, we need more room anyway."

Morgan said, "Where do you think we should go, Pa? What's the timber like around here? Could we go up in the woods?"

"Maybe."

Reuben shifted his chew and said, "How's the water up there?"

"Not too good. What there is, is on the Rocking Chair W."

"How about backtracking on Crystal Creek? Isn't there a cut out about six miles from home?"

"No, you're thinking about a place along Stoney Creek."

"Yeah, that's right."

Tom said, "Hey."

"What?"

"Let's just go home."

Late that afternoon, Al Bluebox had cut Tom's trail. He knew it wasn't what he was looking for, but he followed it for two miles. He knew it was someone strange. He was a half-breed, too, like the woman, but he was mostly Apache. His father had ridden with Cochise. He had scouted himself for the Army down in New Mexico for ten years.

He was stolid, and patient, and skilled at tracking, and cold-blooded. He didn't care much for anyone, white or Indian. He had no loyalties. When he worked, he worked for his wages, that was all. He didn't care who paid him. He could quit the next day and work for the other side without having to sit down and think it over.

He was content right now. Dahlman paid him good money, and didn't care how he did his job—just so he got results. And Al Bluebox was good at that. He was good at getting results.

He came across a line camp. A young cowboy was repairing a pump handle over an old well.

Al slid off his horse. He wore moccasins, and had a bandana tied around his forehead under his hat. He was direct. "Were you talking to this man?" He pointed to the tracks going down past the camp.

"Yeah. Near noon." He felt uncomfortable. He didn't like the Apache. If he had to work around him often, he would have headed back to Montana the next day.

"Who was he?"

"Some drifter. Passing through."

That's what he thought. It was one horse, not two, and whoever was riding it was no trapper. That was a cow pony. It was what he expected to find.

"You see anybody else?"

"No. Just him and you since last Wednesday."

"He say anything?"

"No."

"Say where he was going?"

"No."

Al Bluebox got back on his horse. He would learn more looking than talking. He wasn't going to find out anything more here.

He didn't say good-bye; he just left.

He followed the trail for a while, then left it and swung a wide circle east. He knew where the cowboy was going. He could find him later if he wanted him. He was heading straight as an arrow for the Crystal Creek area. That damn Kiowa woman had a dugout down there. He had promised himself to put a bullet between her eyes some day, after he finished talking to her for a day and a half. She was bad medicine.

He checked the sun and made up his mind. He'd swing a circle as far as the ferry and work his way back in the morning. He'd take a look and see if the cowboy stayed overnight with the Kiowa woman. If he did, maybe he'd shoot both of them.

Frank made the decision. They'd leave in the morning. He found the woman outside, alone, and told her.

She said, "When you go, I will no longer be responsible for you."

"You did a good job. You got me back on my feet. I'll recommend you to all my friends, to anybody who ever gets shot in the leg."

"Be careful."

"If I'm not, do you promise to take me back?"

She put her hand flat on his chest and said, "I will take you back." And she slipped away.

They were packed early in the morning. When they were ready to go, the woman was nowhere in sight.

The girl said, "She won't come back until you're gone."

Frank went back in the dugout and put one of his shirts on her bed under the blanket. He told the girl he'd come back for it sometime.

They all swung up, walked their horses across the creek, and headed out across open country. They rode spread out. They didn't talk much. Tom whistled a little.

CHAPTER 11

Al Bluebox missed them by an hour. He approached the dugout just thinking about the cowboy and the woman. Then he saw the signs of the two other horses he had been hunting.

Damn, he thought. He saw them lead into the dugout, and he saw the fresh tracks going out. He slipped off his horse and into the dugout with his gun in his hand, looking for the woman. She wasn't there. The place was empty.

He got his horse and picked up the fresh tracks. There were four horses. The cowboy was with them, and that irritated him. He realized he had been wasting his time, but brushed it off. He'd follow them now. He'd catch up to them, and he'd get them, one at a time. It shouldn't be too hard. He'd come back for the woman later.

He stayed on their trail until he was certain where they were headed, and then rode off, taking a short cut. They were staying along the grazing land and he could pick them up easily later on the other side of the range. They were going to come down across Crystal Creek, where Dahlman had burned out one of the small ranchers.

He made good time. He picked up the hour head start

they had. When he reached Crystal Creek, he saw them on the other side. They were coming down near the blackened ruins of the house and stable.

He stayed back up off a ridge and slid out his rifle. He'd go for the card player first, the gunfighter. Then he'd go for the trapper. The old man and the cowboy would pose no problem. They could wait their turn. He definitely wanted to get the gunfighter first; after that, it should be easy.

When they reached the edge of the ranch, they all had mixed feelings. It brought back a lot of memories. The burned timbers of the house lay where they had fallen; nothing had been touched since that night. The fence was gone and so was the corral, but the outlines of the house and stable were still visible.

They stopped first on a slight rise and looked down over the place where they had all grown up. Frank finally said, "Well, we did it once. We can do it again."

Tom said, "Let's get a wagon and haul in some lumber from town and do it right. Let's not stick up a pole roof and rough sides just to get something done quick."

Frank said, "That suits me."

Reuben moved a little closer to Morgan and said, softly, "Did you see him?"

"Yeah. I picked him up about a mile ago. He's up there on the ridge."

Frank said, "I think it's that damn Apache Dahlman's got. He rides a horse like that."

Tom said, "You mean there's somebody up there?"

Reuben said, "Sit tight. I'll be right back."

"Reuben," Tom said, "don't take all day."

Morgan said, "Let's go down to the house. He'll have to come a little closer if he wants to be sure."

Frank said, "I imagine Reuben's done this before."

"I imagine," said Morgan.

Tom said, "I hope so."

Al Bluebox saw one of them leave. It was the trapper. He didn't like that. Maybe he was going after supplies, and could be trailed and picked off first.

No—he didn't like that idea. He'd better stay with what he had. He could go get the other one later.

The Apache worked closer, staying low. He saw them ride down to the charred ruins, and he knew he would have to work even closer. It would be too touchy from there, and they were spread out.

Now they had gotten down and were on foot, looking around. That damn gunfighter was on the far side of his horse, and he had trouble getting a good look at him. He slipped forward a little more, dropped to one knee, and brought up the rifle and aimed it. He couldn't get the gunfighter in his sights. The old man was just as bad. He'd have to take the cowboy first. He was right out in the open.

He steadied the rifle and aimed.

"No."

He heard the word and stopped. He didn't move; he knew who it was—the trapper. He had been sitting around a lot lately and hadn't done that much for the last six months, but he hadn't realized he had gotten this care-less.

He waited, absolutely still. He waited until he heard the trapper start down toward him. Then he spun to snap off a shot. He was damn good with a rifle; always had been. As he spun around, he saw Reuben off to his right. He wasn't where he was supposed to be.

He was still trying to figure out how Reuben had done it when the Sharps went off. The bullet virtually tore him in half.

Frank Cameron thought, Tom's right: We'll put this thing back up again and put it up to stay. Then he told Tom, since he knew something about cows, that *they* would start on the house and he could start locating their stock, weed them out from the Circle C cows and get them back where they belonged.

He looked at the three of them and said, "We'll make ourselves at home. Right from the beginning, we'll be-have like we intend to stay—put ourselves back in busi-ness. Let Dahlman make the first move. He can either let us alone or try to run us off. If he lets us alone, good. If he tries to run us off, we'll let Morgan come up with another good suggestion. Now let's go into town and get a wagon."

Calendar was quiet when they rode in. They went over to the livery stable and dickered for a wagon. Morgan told the man, "You set the price, we got the money."

They took the wagon up the street to a store and

bought lumber, nails, and tar paper. They also stocked up on cooking supplies. As they loaded the wagon they knew people were looking at them. The storekeeper was edgy while they shopped.

Doc Kruger walked over. "Frank, someone told me you were in town. Most of them thought you were dead. Or, if you weren't before, you soon will be."

"I've got a good doctor."

"What are you planning on doing?"

"Rebuilding my house."

"You're going back?"

"I am back."

"You'll need a good doctor."

"Then stick around."

"Dahlman won't let you do this. Does he know yet that you're back?"

"I don't think so."

Just then about twenty riders came into town. They came down the main street together, relaxed, talking, heading for the saloon. They came past the store and went on by. They pulled up in front of the saloon, got down, and crowded in.

Doc Kruger looked at Frank. "Well, Dahlman will know now. I think they got a good look at you. If not, someone told me you were here, and someone will tell them."

Tom said to his father, "Do you want me to go ask them to keep it to themselves?"

Reuben said, "Let Morgan do it, he's an old friend."

Frank said to Kruger, "Doc, you can't stop water from

running downhill. Dahlman's going to find out sometime. If not today, then tomorrow. I've made my decision. When he finds out, then he'll have to make his."

They had finished loading. Frank said good-bye, and they started home. The storekeeper came outside and watched. He said, "Doc, is he really going back out in the valley?"

"I believe he is."

"Dahlman won't like that."

"No, he won't. And this time he won't shoot him in the leg."

Dahlman found out after supper. Some of the riders came back from town and told Floyd, and he went up to the house and told Dahlman.

"Cameron was in town."

"The old man?"

"Yeah. Only he don't look that old, they say. He was getting some lumber—told someone he was going to re-build his house."

"Fat chance of that."

"His sons are with him."

"What sons?"

"He's got three sons. They all came home. They were with him. So there are four of them."

"Four? Altogether?"

"Yeah."

"Floyd, I think he's going to need more than four."

"You want me to do anything?"

"Not right now. I want to take care of this Prescott

matter. Let the old geezer pound a few boards together. Let people get used to the idea that he's there. We'll go over next week."

About an hour later, Red was at the door with Floyd. Floyd said, "I think you better hear this."

Red said, "You remember those two I had trouble with in town last night? The guy playing cards and the trapper?"

"Yeah."

"They were with Cameron today. I spotted them when we came into town. They were loading a wagon at the store."

Dahlman looked at Floyd. Floyd said, "They must be two of Cameron's boys."

"What did the other one look like?"

Red said, "Not much. Looked like someone you wouldn't even think twice about putting in one of the line camps. He wasn't even wearing a gun."

"They were with Cameron?"

"As thick as thieves. They were all loading the wagon. They talked a little with Doc Kruger, and then they all left town together."

"But there were just four of them?"

"That's all I saw. I kept my eye on them from the saloon. I figured you didn't want me doing anything without talking to you."

Floyd said, "Do you want me to send someone over there and take a look? See what they're doing?"

"I know what they're doing. What I don't know is why. You sure that old man ain't senile?"

Red said, "He don't look that old. Not from where I was standing. He looked a hell of a lot better than he did the night we ran him off. I noticed him limping a little, but he was still moving pretty good."

"But there was still only four damn people, right?"

"Right."

"No one else?"

"No, not what I could see."

"I'm not going to waste any time worrying about four people. Look, Floyd, send someone to go over and take a look, but have him stay back. I don't want him doing anything more than just looking. If he sees ten or fifteen riders come in and bed down, tell him to get back here right away. But if all he can count are four, then tell him to stay right where he is. After we take care of Prescott, we'll go talk to Cameron."

It nagged him a little, but not much. He kept coming back to the fact that there were only four of them. Even if they were all dangerous men, it didn't matter. He had close to seventy-five men right now and could go over a hundred in a week if he had to.

You don't have to shoot too straight in a situation like that, just often.

Two hours later, a line rider came in leading a horse with a man tied over the back. He was dead.

Floyd came to the door. "It's the Apache."

"Bluebox?"

"Yeah."

"What happened?"

"Someone put a slug into him, flush in the stomach."

"Where?"

"Crystal Creek, on Box C land. And whoever it was used a Sharps."

"A buffalo gun?"

"Yeah. I think it was the trapper."

"You mean Cameron."

"That's right. I think it was Cameron."

Dahlman said, "Okay, someone got the Apache. But there are still only four of them, right?"

"Yeah," Floyd said, "but I think they are four damn good ones."

"Well, we'll still take care of Prescott first."

He didn't second guess himself. He wasn't given to doubts. He had always been forceful, positive. When he wanted something, he was hell bent until he got it.

When he was sixteen, his father was badly hurt in an accident breaking a horse. He died three days later. Dahlman didn't waste any time mourning. He took the five hundred cows they had and drove them himself to Dodge and sold them. Then he went back to Texas and bought more stock. He also scrounged the brush and picked up strays, never overly concerned as to how much the cow had strayed. He worked up a herd of nine hundred cows this time, hired a few hands, and drove to Dodge again.

When he was eighteen, he was shot in the back and left for dead by three men he had just hired. They took off with his herd. It took him two days to get a horse and three weeks to travel far enough to track them down. He hung all three himself, one at a time, from the end of a wagon tongue.

He came up to Wyoming for the land. He built up his herd and spread out over more and more grazing land. He cleaned out all the Indians he could find and annexed as much water as he could.

When he was thirty, he took a vacation and went to St. Louis. He made a few good friends and dabbled in stock speculations, considered going into real estate ventures and railroad construction, and made one disastrous attempt to get into politics. He finally came back home to build up his ranch. He found nesters and a sudden rash of small ranchers.

What he had long considered to be open range was fast disappearing. He sat down, mapped out a plan, brought in the men he needed, and began cleaning out again. He extended the Circle C ranch in all four directions, determined to build a solid base of power this time. Everyone in his way would be run over. He was not used to taking no for an answer. He was a powerful, wealthy, ruthless man.

He thought about Frank Cameron. He might have made a mistake. Maybe he should have hung him that night, but he wasn't going to look back. He'd hang him this time, or shoot him, or both. *Something*, but it would be permanent.

It just made him a little uneasy seeing Al Bluebox come back strapped across a horse. Hell, Bluebox was good. He was an Apache—half of him, anyway, the half that counted. And an Apache, even half of one, was good before he was two years old.

But there were only four of them. Nothing to worry about, not really. However, it never hurt to do things right. He decided he'd send for Nate Lovelace.

CHAPTER 12

They put in a good week. They got the walls up and the house under a roof. Tom had kept busy, and he had well over a hundred head of Box C cows back on their own range. It was a beginning.

The week had been especially good for Frank. It gave him a chance to get a good look at his sons, and he was not disappointed. He was beginning to feel sorry for Dahlman if he came around looking for trouble.

But, though his boys were good, he didn't get carried away. He knew they didn't stand a chance in hell in any match-off with Dahlman's riders, no matter how good they were.

He knew they had only one chance—to get Dahlman. The trick was, to get Dahlman before he got any of his sons. The ranch was not worth losing even one of them. He knew they should leave—he also knew he couldn't.

They had all spotted the rider Dahlman sent out ten minutes after he got there. He worked to stay out of sight, but it didn't work. They knew where he was morning, afternoon, and night.

Reuben said, "Dahlman must be busy. All we rate right now is a watchdog."

Tom said, "That's all right with me."

Frank said, "I don't guess it was personal then when he came over and burned me out. It must have just been business. Otherwise, he'd have been back by now."

Morgan rolled a cigarette and said, "There must be someone else he wants burned out worse than you."

"Well, we'll have to be patient. I'm sure he'll get around to us when he can."

Two days later, Tom ran some cows over near the stakeout. He waved a friendly greeting and yelled as the man pulled back, trying to get out of sight.

"Wait." He got the cows started down the long slope towards the creek and pulled up. "Hey, are you thirsty?"

There was no answer.

Tom said, "Come on over. Jesus, you must be tired sitting up here watching us. Do you want some good spring water?"

The man didn't move.

Tom held up both hands. "I never carry a gun, and I sure as hell ain't going to try and wrestle you." He got down, hunkered on his heels, and fished out the Bull Durham sack. He held it up. "You want some makings?"

The man came out then, carefully, looking around. He was young, and had blond hair. He was trying to grow a mustache. "Do you really have spring water?"

"Yeah." He handed him the water. "Where are you from?"

"Nebraska."

"You been with the Circle C long?"

"Six months."

"It's a big spread. I was with the Bar T, and I thought we were big."

"You were with the Bar T? Charles Collins' ranch? In Oklahoma?"

"Yeah."

"I'll be a sheepherder's dog. My brother works for them."

"You're kidding. What's his name?"

"Ed Burns."

"Pancakes Ed?"

"Yeah, that's his name. Pancakes Ed."

"I know him. He made two good drives for me. He knows more about shoeing horses than anyone I ever saw. I never had a lame horse in the three years he was with us."

The cowboy pointed his finger. "Wait a minute. You're not Tom Cameron. Oh my God, you are, aren't you? You're Mr. Collins' foreman. Ed told my pa about you. Pa wanted me to go to the Bar T and get a job. He said it would be a good place for me to learn something. I figured I would, but first I thought I'd look around a little, sow a few wild oats."

"If you ever want a job with the Bar T, all you got to do is tell them you're Pancakes Ed's brother."

He looked around and said, seriously, "You can't stay here. Your pa knows that, don't he? I mean, you got good grass and water, but Mr. Dahlman ain't like Mr. Collins. We got a lot of people working for us who ain't interested in working with cows. They're planning on running you

off. That's why I'm here. I'm supposed to be watching
you. I'm supposed to let them know if you hire anybody
or get any help. Soon as he gets the chance, Mr. Dahlman
is going to come over here and run you off. I don't think
he knows who you are."

"You don't have to sit up here and watch us. Hell,
come on down where there's some decent shade. If you
get thirsty, help yourself to the spring. We won't feed
you, not pancakes anyway, but you're welcome to make
yourself at home."

"I mean it, they can get nasty. Maybe you better tell
your pa."

"I'll tell him," Tom said.

"You want me to say something to him?"

"No, I'll tell him."

Tom got up on his horse.

The cowboy said, "I was thinking about moving on."

Tom waved and started down the slope, and the cowboy yelled a little louder, "I was going to go last week.
I'm just finishing out the month. I never did like it here."
He stepped closer, cupped his hands to his mouth and
yelled, "Maybe I'll head for the Bar T now! I already
seen St. Louie!"

He watched as Tom waved again and rode flat out
down the slope with a yelp and a laugh. He said, in a flat
voice, knowing Tom couldn't hear him anymore, "Hey,
don't wait too long. Go back to Mr. Collins. Don't stay
here."

Another week went by and they still hadn't heard anything from the Circle C.

"He must be busy," Reuben observed.

Frank said, "I'd hate to think he don't want to bother with us, that we're not worth the time."

Tom said, "The man is more than busy. I know what it's like. He's got records to keep, payrolls to meet, calves to brand, fences to mend . . ."

Morgan said, "And nesters to burn."

Frank said, "He's waiting for something, which isn't like him. Usually he'd just come over here and kick us the hell off."

"Maybe we should go over there."

Tom said, "I'm satisfied to wait."

They had finished the house and gotten the corral up, and Tom had built the herd back up to almost three hundred head. They had not been wasting any time.

They went back into town for more supplies. They got there at noon, and Frank saw the Kiowa woman across the street. He handed the list to Tom and told him he'd be back.

He crossed the street and said, "Tia."

She stood still and waited until he walked up.

He said, "How are you?"

"All right. How are you?"

"Walking better. I could probably run if I had a reason."

"You look good."

"A lot better than I did the night Henry dumped me in your lap."

She almost smiled. "You smell better, too."

"You think so?"

"I think so."

"Have you been left alone?"

"Yes. I don't think I'm the one the Circle C is interested in."

"So far he hasn't bothered me either."

"Don't let that fool you."

"I'm not. I know he's coming sometime. If it wasn't for that, I'd ask you to move in with us."

She looked at him.

"Once this is over, once it's settled, I want you to get out of that place and move in with me. I don't want you over there anymore."

"Frank, he's going to burn you out again."

"Maybe."

"He will. You're a bug in the road that he's going to step on. Go somewhere else, please."

He smiled. "Don't you think I can do it?"

She looked at him, deadly serious, and said, "No."

They finished loading the wagon, and Reuben and Morgan were thinking about getting a beer when fifteen Circle C riders came into town, riding together. They pulled up to the saloon, crowding up to the rail, with three of them turning off and riding over to the stagecoach station, leading an empty horse. One of them was Red.

Tom said, "I think I'll skip my beer."

Frank said, "I think we all will."

Reuben said, "Just one?"

"No, not now," said Frank.

"We have to sometime."

Morgan said, "It is hot and I am thirsty."

Tom said, "It doesn't seem hot to me."

The stage came racing into town just then, kicking up dust. It stopped to unload, the horses stamping and blowing. Two women, a drummer, and a solitary man got off.

The three riders for the Circle C went up to the man and they stood there talking for a minute. He was tall, and dressed well: low-crown hat, long coat, white shirt, trousers tucked into long, shiny, expensive, black boots. They got his war bag and he swung up on the horse they were leading and all of them swung down the street.

As they came past the wagon, the tall man suddenly stopped and looked over. He said softly, "Morgan, is that you?"

"Hello, Nate."

"It's been a long time."

"You just passing through, Nate?"

"I'm always just passing through."

Morgan said, "You're keeping bad company."

Red spun his horse around and started to speak, but Nate held up his hand. "I've been told that before."

"You're looking well."

"So are you, Morgan. I missed you at Waco."

"You didn't miss me. You hung back until you knew I was gone."

Nate smiled. "Whoever told you that is a liar."

Morgan took a slight, almost imperceptible step to one side. He said, flatly, "I'm the one telling you."

"If I wasn't in a hurry, I'd buy you a drink. Maybe later."

"Anytime."

They rode off.

Tom said, "Well, we know now what Dahlman's been waiting for."

They got back to the ranch, unloaded the wagon, and turned the horses out into the corral.

Frank said, "We might as well go over this again."

Reuben put a chew in his mouth and sat back up against the side of the house in the shade. Tom hunkered down and scratched in the dirt with a small stick. Morgan stood at the end of the house and rolled a cigarette.

"First, Dahlman is not going to let us stay here. It's not good business and it's no good for his pride. He'll get around to us, you can be sure of that. He's got, let's say, seventy-five men. Probably half of them would show up here some night if he told them to, maybe more. The rest would rather stay out of it.

"There are four of us. We can't expect any help from the law, since Lee Moncrief never leaves his office, let alone Calendar. I don't think that man can see ten feet in front of himself anymore. Henry might come back—so might Christmas. That would give us five, but I don't think that's going to do it. And now Dahlman's brought in Nate Lovelace, who I guess is a professional gunfighter. How good is he, Morgan?"

"Good. Earp left Dodge for a while because of Nate.

He is a pure killer. He shoots either a handgun or a rifle equally well. He's good at his business."

"Why do you think Dahlman sent for him? If I had fifty men to use to burn out four, I wouldn't waste my money getting any more. Not at his price."

"I think Reuben shooting the Apache has spooked him a little. He's probably being careful."

"Dahlman don't spook," Frank said. "Hell, he'd come over here by himself if he had no other way. He don't run scared. He's used to reaching out and taking."

"You got to remember he burned you out once, and you came back. He isn't used to that. If I were in his shoes and somebody I burned out came back and was weeding out his cows again and building his house back up and all he had was four men, I'd wonder what he knew. It's one thing being a fool, and another thing knowing exactly what you're doing. He has to at least consider that we just might know what we're doing."

"Do we?" Frank asked.

"No."

"You think we should pull up and leave, Morgan?"

"No. I'm here now. I'll leave when it's my idea."

"What about you, Reuben?"

Reuben chewed a little and said, "I got nowhere to go right now."

"Tom?"

"There's got to be one person in this family who's smart enough to know when to go. You sure we never had a sister?"

Frank said, "If we're going to stay, does anyone have any idea how we ought to do this?"

Tom said, "That's Reuben's department. He's used to staying alive all by himself with Comanches, Kiowa, Shoshoni, and Cheyenne all around him. He must know something."

"Yes. Make sure you're lucky."

Frank said, "You three are a big help. After this conversation, I will definitely sleep better tonight."

Tom said, "Morgan, you said Nate Lovelace is good."

"He is."

"How good are you?"

Morgan said, evenly, "I'm better."

That night, Frank Cameron walked down to the corral. It was a dark, quiet night. He stood with one foot up on the fence. The night air smelled sweet.

He tried to think of something they could do. He didn't like the idea of waiting for Dahlman to make a move and then simply trying to defend themselves. He wanted to take the initiative, but he couldn't think of anything that made sense—that had any hope of working.

He wanted to quit. That's what he really wanted to do. He wanted to get his sons out of there. He wanted them to go back where they came from. He didn't want them hurt.

Reuben came up out of the night in his shirt sleeves. He leaned on the fence and said, "It's a pretty night, ain't it?"

"Yes."

"When I was up in the mountains, we used to have nights sometimes so pretty you didn't want to sleep. It was good for the soul just to sit out and watch, to store it up for the bad days when nothing went right."

"I know what you mean. Overall, it ain't a bad life."

"No. There are parts of it that are pretty bad, but if you go about it right, if you keep your eyes and ears open and look around, it isn't bad all the time. There are parts of it that make up for a lot."

"There were times when you three boys were small, when you were all here at home, that I was very happy. I had your mother and I had you three, and I wished life could just stop and stay like that forever."

"It doesn't."

"No, it doesn't."

"Did you know, Pa, that I was married once?"

"No."

"She was a Shoshoni. We married ourselves up in the mountains. You would have liked her. I thought a couple of times about the two of us coming home here for a visit. I was serious about it, but I just put it off too long. I should have gone and done it."

"Your mother would have liked that."

"She was killed. It was pretty bad for me for a while. You know, though, Pa, what would have been worse? If we had never met. Or, if she had turned out to be deceitful or miserable."

He looked at his father and said, "There are a lot of things worse than having someone you love die." He took a deep breath and said, "Good night, Pa," and then walked off.

Frank stood there a moment and then realized there was someone else off to his right in the dark.

Tom stepped closer and said, "I never heard Reuben talk so much."

"Neither did I."

"And make as much sense. Good night, Pa."

Frank stood there until he was gone. Then he said, "Morgan? I guess you're out here somewhere, too, aren't you?"

Slowly, a figure came toward him from the end of the corral. He was carrying a rifle. "Hello, Pa."

"Is anybody sleeping?"

Morgan said, "Yeah. Probably Dahlman."

CHAPTER 13

It started to rain before Nate Lovelace reached the ranch, and they rode the last two miles through a steady shower. Dahlman was waiting for them and he took Nate into the house. Floyd came along. The three had a drink.

Nate Lovelace sat on a chair near the desk and said, "I got a good look at the Camerons in town."

"They were there?"

"All of them, getting supplies."

"All four?"

"All four." He threw off his drink neatly and said, "Do you know who Morgan Cameron is?"

"Who?"

"He was with the Hawk in Tombstone. They were together a couple of years. Morgan is better than the Hawk. Believe me."

"You mean he's a gunfighter?"

"The man is a gambler, a connoisseur of fine wines, good-looking women, good horseflesh, and absolutely the wrong person to insult with a gun in your hand."

"Does he know you?"

"He knows me."

"Can you take him?"

"That remains to be seen. It is a question I've asked myself from time to time."

"You're going to try?"

"Under the right circumstances." He held out his glass for a refill. "That rain gave me a slight chill. Do you know who his brother is?"

"Which one?"

"Tom Cameron, his younger brother. He is the top honcho for the Bar T, for Charles Collins. You've heard of Charles Collins, haven't you? Well, Collins turned the whole thing over to Cameron a couple of years ago. He apparently knows cows like I know guns. If you had a man like that, you wouldn't have to burn anyone out. He's made a lot of money for Collins. How did you happen to pick this family to decide to do business with?"

Dahlman ignored him and said evenly, "What about the other brother? I don't suppose he owns the railroad or anything, does he?"

"I know nothing about that one. I wouldn't assume, though, that he's a saddle tramp."

"Is this job going to be too big for you?"

"No."

"There are still only four of them over there, no matter who the hell they are."

"You're right."

"Well, I don't propose to challenge them to a duel. If it were the only way, I'd go over there with my bare hands and throw them off the damn place. But I intend to use what I have—power, money, seventy-five riders drawing my money, and one first-class, highly recommended, well-versed shooter."

"Just don't expect a cakewalk."

"Are you ready to go to work?"

"You're the boss."

Dahlman put down his glass. He said, "Floyd, I don't want any nesters, sheepherders, or penny-ante ranchers crowding my cows, tramping my grass, or fencing off my water. I won't put up with it. I ran a two-bit rummy off Crystal Creek once, and he's back there again. He is my next item of business, and here's what I want done."

He looked at Nate Lovelace. "You go into Calendar. Get a room at the hotel—makes a nice place to spend a few days. Play cards, have a drink, make yourself visible. I will pay all expenses. I want you there twenty-four hours a day, seven days a week. One week should do it. If any member of the Cameron family—and that includes the boy rancher and the connoisseur of fine wines—comes into town, make sure they don't leave. I'll give you, in addition to all expenses, five hundred dollars for the week and a thousand bonus for each Cameron you shoot. I don't care if you shoot them in the back. I look only for results."

He turned back to Floyd. "Tomorrow, take all those expensive guns that came up here from Texas, those Mormon cousins from Utah, those four big mouths who said they rode with Quantrell, and go over to Crystal Creek. Find out how tough a nut that is to crack."

"You want me to run them out?"

"I'm not sending you over there to check their tally books. Don't make this any bigger than it is."

"Okay."

"Floyd?"

"What?"

"If you can't do it, come back and tell me. I'll do it myself."

Frank Cameron was up early. He stepped outside and stretched and got some water to wash up. The early morning air was cool; they were headed for some cold weather.

He heard Reuben get up and stoke up the fire in the cook stove. He finished washing, put his hat back on and looked past the corral, out over the open range. The horses were quiet. He could see some cows getting up and moving around about a half mile away. He was pleased with the work Tom had done. They were back in business again. His leg was a little stiff yet, but he didn't think about it too much. He could move pretty good once he was up and around.

He could smell some coffee. He took a last look around, and decided they should be able to finish the stable by afternoon. Maybe he would send Reuben after some firewood, get started on that while the weather was holding. He wondered if Dahlman was up yet. He didn't think it was right that one person could cause so much misery for so many others. He decided that if he didn't get word from him by the end of the week, he'd go over there and do something.

Floyd Walker had had a bad night. He'd had some indigestion, didn't sleep well, and was moving slow when he got up. He went light on breakfast, and ended up drinking two cups of coffee and smoking a cigarette.

He passed the word around to be ready to leave by ten. It ended up being closer to eleven, since he had to wait for some riders to come in from one of the camps.

One of the Mormon cousins said, "Hell, why wait, we'll go ourselves, there's only four of them. Jesus, we've got thirty guys sitting out there now getting in each other's way. What are we doing waiting for some more?"

Floyd said, "Just make sure you don't hang back once we get there. I didn't see you looking too anxious over at Prescott's."

Dahlman came down once to see what was holding them up. Floyd caught hell, passed it on to the last rider pulling out, and they were gone by eleven. Someone counted as they went by: fifty-two, and all of them like bonus money.

Nate Lovelace reached Calendar before noon. He left the horse at the livery stable and walked over to the hotel. He checked in, went up to his room, and unpacked his bag. He liked things orderly, and didn't leave much to chance. He liked to have all the odds in his favor; he never counted on being lucky—he counted on being ready.

He had not yet thought through, though, what he would do if Morgan Cameron came into town. He had wondered about it, but he hadn't reached a decision. It was a loose end that bothered him. If anyone else came into town, he'd make money. He was sure of that.

He went downstairs and into the dining room. He shared a long table with seven other people. The food was all right. He had had better, but it was done and out of the way.

He walked over to the saloon. The crowd was slim. There were games at only two tables. One woman was hanging around, looking hung over. He took his time and sized up the room, judging it from different angles.

He found the best location, but a drummer was sitting in that chair, playing poker. It took him only a minute to convince him to move. He took over the chair, sat down, got some chips, bit the tip off a good cigar, checked the front door, and settled down to waiting.

When Reuben finished breakfast, Frank said, "Why don't you go find some firewood? You bring it in and Morgan and I will cut and stack it."

Tom said, "I saw some good hickory, oak, and maple. A lot of fallen trees. All you can haul. It's out about five miles."

Reuben said all right, hitched the wagon, got an ax, fixed a chew, and left within an hour. He was back with a full load by ten. He unloaded, got a drink, and took a little time to repair the tailgate.

When he started away from the ranch for another load, he was headed due west, in the direction of the Circle C. It was eleven o'clock.

In the middle of the morning, Tom was clearing out some rough brush country at the far end of the ranch, cutting Box C stock from Circle C, when his horse threw a shoe.

He got down and checked the hoof, then he walked back, found the shoe and patched the thing together. He decided to go on into town. They were short on shoes at the ranch, and he figured he might as well take care of that now and pick up some nails, too. He was not close to the house, and it wasn't that much farther to town.

He'd have to take his time and baby the horse, but it was a pretty day. He figured he'd get there about two o'clock. A little late for lunch, but maybe he could find something to eat anyway.

A wheel was going bad. He'd have to take it off and fix it after he got this load in; he wasn't going to fool with it now. It had begun squealing about a mile out from the ranch and he had considered going back, but he had taken a look at it and decided to keep going, get one more load, and then pull the wheel.

Reuben had never cared much for wagons. He had no time for them, and almost preferred walking. He was crossing hilly country, going down one hill and up another, shifting his weight, sifting signs, always looking around. He was thinking of the mountains, getting tired of ranching, thinking about trapping again. He was glad to see his brothers and his pa, and it was a change, but now he was getting restless, anxious to be on the move. The places he had been, the sights he had seen, so much bleakness and beauty, it had made him the man he was. He had seen emptiness and loneliness, sounds and colors, the cold, the snow, the sun, the clear waters of mountain lakes—all these things were now a part of him. It was something no one could ever take away. He was a unique person, and he knew it. He knew what he had done in his lifetime, what he had seen and heard, and there was little now that threatened him. Each day was a day to be lived as well as possible.

He had been aware of a problem for twenty minutes now. Something wasn't right. When he finally stopped the wagon, he sat still for a long time. He pulled the tobacco out of his pocket and bit off a sizable chew, worked it around until it was just right, spit once to test it, and flicked the reins. The horse started again.

He shrugged his shoulders. It was too late to go back. Besides, he could run back faster than he could go in the wagon. He watched a flock of birds, and noticed a fox heading for the woods. He was getting close now. Whatever it was, it was just over the next hill.

He topped the hill and took a look. Sitting in a long line, about a quarter of a mile away on top of the *next* hill, watching him, were Circle C cowboys. He knew they were Circle C; he didn't know there were fifty-two of them, but he knew there were enough. They had all they needed. They were sitting there, watching him, waiting. They didn't have to hurry.

He got off the wagon, unhitched the horse, and gave a shove and turned the wagon over on its side. He got the Sharps and his possibles sack and dug out the boxes of shells he carried. He took the horse about fifty feet down below the top of the hill, away from the riders, and tied it fast. That would be his last resort.

He came back to the wagon, and sat down behind it. He loaded the Sharps and waited. He knew they could go around him or right over him, but that was their problem, it was out of his hands. Either way, he was ready.

Floyd's stomach was a little better. He put it out of his mind and concentrated on the job to be done. They had spotted the wagon slowly crossing the hills about ten minutes ago and had stopped to wait for it.

"You think it's one of them?"

Floyd said, "It's one of them."

One of the Mormon cousins said, "You want me to take him?"

"Not yet. Let him get closer. I want to see which one it is." He wasn't sure whether he wanted it to be Morgan or not. He had mixed feelings.

When the wagon topped the last hill and stopped, someone said, "It's the trapper."

They watched him turn over the wagon, get the horse out of range and come back.

"Cool son of a gun, ain't he?"

"He knows who we are."

"It don't take brains to tell that."

The Mormon cousin said, "Should we just ride right over him?"

Floyd said, "I thought you wanted to take him yourself?"

"Not with him holding onto that Sharps."

One of the other Mormon cousins said, "We can take him together. The five of us."

"Hell, yes."

Floyd said, "I don't want it to take all day."

"It won't take ten minutes."

"That's what I'm giving you."

"Do we get a bonus if we have him out to dry in five?"

"Yeah."

They spread out, gave a war yell, and suddenly raced down off the hill and up the other side towards the wagon.

Reuben's first shot knocked a rider off his horse; his second shot knocked horse and rider both down. His third shot caught one of them changing his mind and swerving away. He let the other two ride past the wagon, yelling, firing, and missing. He knelt down with his hand gun and picked both of them off at close range as they rode past.

Then it was quiet.

Reuben reloaded the Sharps and the handgun and waited.

Someone said, "Hey, Floyd, you going to give him a bonus?"

Someone else said, "The Mormons won't care."

Floyd had expected them to have trouble, but he didn't expect what he had just seen. Holy hell, he didn't miss a shot. He only fired five times, but picked them all off on the run. Floyd didn't think he'd try that again.

He said, "Let's go get him. Spread out. And don't shoot each other."

He waved his hand and they started down the hill together, slowly, deliberately. The Sharps was fired and one of them went down at that distance. It fired again and another went down. They broke into a run, spreading out more, some of them opening up fire too soon, a little spooked.

Reuben was down behind the wagon. He had a good spot. He fired quickly, methodically, doing just what he wanted to do, picking off the right one at the right time. He had survived a rush by twenty Comanches once, thought he had been damn lucky, didn't know now that there were fifty-two Circle C riders. He did know there were a hell of a lot more than the twenty Comanches.

As they came up the hill toward him, they were slowed down, off-balanced, at a disadvantage. It was hard to fire accurately. The center of the line was soon broken by the deadly fire of the Sharps, and now he was using the handgun as they were close. Suddenly they pulled back and went off to regroup.

He had been nicked on the shoulder and something had creased his forehead, but otherwise he was all right.

They pulled up and looked around. Someone took a quick count. "We lost ten."

"Maybe it'd be cheaper to pay him off."

One of the Texans said, "Maybe if we asked him nicely, he'd go away."

Floyd knew they couldn't keep this up. They were going to get him, he knew that, but he didn't want to lose too many more men. They hadn't even gotten close to the ranch yet.

"Everybody get down. Move in a little. Pick a good spot, and pour in a steady fire. I don't want one spoke left on that damn wagon. Let's go."

They pulled their rifles and walked their horses in closer in a wide line and then got down and began firing.

Reuben dug in. He had no choice. He couldn't return their fire. He dug in as deep as he could, down under the wagon. It took a terrible beating. Wood chips flew continuously as slugs ripped away. There was nothing he could do but hang on and wait it out.

They fired for a full ten minutes, until their rifle barrels heated up. Floyd finally waved to them to stop. It was strangely quiet at first after the constant firing.

"Malcolm, take a look. We'll cover you."

One of the riders got up on his horse and slowly descended the hill. He hadn't even started up the other side when a shot rang out and he was knocked off his horse.

Someone said, "I don't think he understands what we're trying to do."

One of the Texans said, laconically, "When do you want us to start covering Malcolm?"

Floyd was getting a headache. He decided not to waste any more time. He didn't care who he lost now. He was definitely going to get him this time, even if he had to go up there and pull him out with his bare hands.

When the heavy firing stopped, Reuben knew someone would be coming. It was something the Comanches would never do. In fact, they would not have lost two men. They would have circled him and waited, even if it took a year. But he knew whoever was running things out there would want to know something right away, so he was ready. The shot was easy to make, like bringing down an old bull buffalo.

But he was hurt. He had been able to stay low, had the wagon on the edge of the hill and could get down back of the ground, but he had taken a lot of fire. He was bleeding along the ribs; one of them was broken, he thought. He could feel it when he breathed. He also had wounds on both arms, and had been clipped in the thigh.

He kept an eye across the hill and got some pressure on his ribs to slow down the bleeding. It would be all right if he didn't have to move too much. It would be better if he could get a tight bandage wrapped around his chest, but he couldn't take the chance right then.

He wondered if they'd get tired and go home. He didn't really think they'd do that, but it would be nice. They'd probably get mad. Whoever was in charge was probably frustrated and furious, and they'd probably do something dumb, like come again and lose some more people. Probably in the process they would get him, which was the part he didn't like.

Oh, hell, he thought, no sense worrying about it. It was out of his hands. He flexed his arm and checked the bleeding. He'd do what he could so it wouldn't be too easy for them.

CHAPTER 14

The blacksmith was around back when Tom stopped. He got down, looked around, then led the horse around the house. Jake Hoover was pushing fifty, a big man, strong, with a stomach starting to assert itself. He wore a full beard and worked with an apron on, no shirt, and a hat. He never took the hat off. He couldn't ride a horse worth a damn. He found that out before he was twenty, so he wasted no time in becoming a blacksmith. He was married for the third time and he had twelve kids between the three women.

"I got a horse with a bad shoe."

"Yeah, I see."

"Are you busy?"

"I better be or my wife comes out that door right there. If I sit down, she's got that door open and wants to know why." He walked over and ran his hand down the horse's leg and raised the foot. "Did you put this back on?"

"Yeah."

"That's not a bad job."

"I got lucky."

"If you want to go across the street for a drink, I'll have this done when you get back."

"I don't want a drink, but I'll get something to eat and be right back." He went out front and up the street.

Nate Lovelace never was a big drinker. He preferred fine food. He didn't expect to find any in Calendar, but that's what he preferred. He just kept a glass of whiskey near him for company to nurse along while playing cards.

The card game was slow, but it helped kill time. He was good at waiting, and he also liked to play cards. He could do it all day. He knew he was intimidating the dealer, just his sitting there, so the challenge was gone. The dealer was underplaying his cards when it came down to a direct confrontation with Nate, and no one else at the table could give him any competition, but it was better than no game at all.

One of the three rummies he had hired for drinks to watch the street for him came in and hurried back to the table, stumbling at the last minute.

"One of the Camerons just come in town."

He took it slow, checking his cards first, then said, "Which one?"

"I don't know."

"What did he look like? Can you tell me that?"

"Young. Looks like a kid. He's the one who laughs a lot. He's at the blacksmith's."

"Was he wearing a low-crown hat?"

"No. He had the kind some of those cowboys up in Montana wear."

So it was Tom Cameron from the Bar T. Too bad. He was a good-looking kid. Even the trapper could be tricky;

not difficult, but tricky. He wondered what the old man would be like? He'd have to remember not to take him for granted—that damn Morgan got his ability from someone.

"Is he alone?"

"Yeah."

He handed him a half dollar. "Get a quick drink and get back out there. Let me know right away if you see anyone else come in." Then, to be sure, "One more time. He was not wearing a flat-brim hat with a low crown? He didn't have his gun tied down low?"

"I told you, his hat's one of those Montana kind. And he don't wear no gun at all."

Nate excused himself from the card game. He left the saloon and went across the street to the General Store.

"I want a gun and holster."

"What kind?"

"Give me that .44 right there."

Cal Coover got the gun out of the case and went around to the other side for a holster. He laid three different kinds onto the counter.

Nate said, "No. I want one gun, one holster, one belt, six bullets. I don't care what kind as long as they all go together."

Cal said, "I don't . . ."

"I'll do it myself." He picked up the gun, slid it into the first holster, reached around the case for a box of cartridges, and dumped them out. He loaded the gun and put it back in the holster. It took him thirty-five seconds.

"Charge all this to Jim Dahlman."

"Did he say . . ." Cal stopped when Nate looked at

him. He started to ask him to sign for them, but thought better of that, too.

Nate walked out.

Cal noticed Lovelace was already wearing a gun. He wondered what he wanted with another one, was tempted to go to the door and see which way he was headed, but didn't do it. Cal Coover was fifty-five. He hadn't lasted that long by looking out the door at the wrong time.

Nate was cautious when he approached the blacksmith shop. Jake Hoover was working on the horse. There was no one else around.

Jake looked up. He didn't like what he saw. He moved back a little toward the corner where he stashed the shotgun.

Nate said, "I'm looking for someone."

"There's no one here."

"He was here just a minute ago."

"I don't know anything about that."

"He's a cowboy. He was talking to you just a minute ago."

"Well, he ain't here now."

"Where did he go?"

"I don't know."

Jake admired the way he did it. It made him nervous, but he admired how Nate suddenly, with almost no effort, had his gun in his hand and pointed straight at him.

Nate said, "You can do better than that."

"He said he'd be back, that's all I know."

Nate simply cocked the gun.

Jake said, "He went to get something to eat."

He put the gun away and headed back out. He stopped and said, "Is that his horse?"

"Yes."

"You don't have to hurry. He won't need it."

He figured he'd try the hotel first. It was the last place he would go to eat after lunch that day, but it was the first place a lot of people went. There were six different places a man in town could sit down and eat without getting sick. Well, at least five.

He'd try the hotel first, then work back down that side of the street. As long as he stayed between him and the blacksmith's shop, Tom wasn't going anywhere.

At noon, Frank Cameron stopped cutting wood and got himself a cup of coffee. He was going to warm up some beans, but he decided to wait for Reuben to get back first. He should be back soon. He was running late.

Frank leaned against the corral fence and sipped coffee from an old tin cup. Morgan walked over and said, "Someone's coming."

"It's not Reuben, not from that direction."

"It's a carriage, not a wagon."

"I think it's Doc Kruger."

They waited until the carriage pulled in off the road. Doc Kruger didn't get down. "I can't stay, Frank. I got a call."

"I hope the guy wasn't shot in the leg."

"I hope he remembers to pay his bill."

"I hope he waits to see if what you're going to do will work or not."

Morgan said, dryly, "Was Pa right? When you fixed his leg, was that the first time you ever practiced medicine?"

"No, Morgan," Frank said, "I told you it *felt* like it."

"You two are funny, but I've got to go. Frank, I saw your other son on my way out."

"Tom?"

"Your youngest. He was heading into town. He said he was going into the blacksmith's; his horse had thrown a shoe."

"Was he carrying the horse?"

"No, the horse was still carrying him."

"He'll be back, I reckon, when he gets done."

"I wouldn't be surprised. Well, I might stop on my way back."

Frank went into the house and dug out his war bag. He scrounged around in it and came up with a gun. He strapped it on. Morgan watched him.

"I haven't seen that gun since I was a kid."

"You used to get it when I wasn't looking and practice with it."

"You knew that?"

"I knew it."

"And you didn't say anything?"

"I did the same thing when I was a boy with my pappy's gun." He went out and carried his saddle over to the corral.

Morgan said, "Where are you going?"

"To find out what's holding up Reuben."

"I'll go."

"No, I need the exercise."

"We'll both go."

He considered that a minute, then Morgan said, "There's someone coming now."

Frank looked. It was a single rider. He was riding at a steady pace, heading straight for the ranch. They didn't recognize him when he pulled up.

He said, "Howdy."

Frank said, "Would you like a cup of coffee?"

"No, thanks. I'm looking for Tom Cameron. Are you his pa?"

"Yeah. He's not here right now."

"We were talking before. My brother is Pancakes Ed. He works for the Bar T. He always spoke good about your son. That's why I stopped. I'm on my way to Montana. I've been working for the Circle C. I quit today, and I wanted to tell him something before I left."

"He went into town. I don't know when he'll be back."

"He can't go into town. He can't do that."

"Why not?"

"Oh my God, Nate Lovelace is there. Mr. Dahlman sent him into town to sit and wait until someone from here comes in."

Morgan said, "Is Lovelace in town right now?"

"I think so. Mr. Dahlman is sending Floyd Walker over here with just about everybody he can get his hands on. Nate Lovelace was supposed to go into town and wait there in case someone came in that way."

"When is Walker coming here?"

"Right now. He was getting ready to leave when I left."

Morgan looked at his father. "What do you think?"

"I think I am going to kill Jim Dahlman. Now we know what's holding up Reuben."

Morgan said, "Let's go."

"No. You go get Tom and take care of Lovelace. I'll go after Reuben."

"Don't go to the Circle C without me."

"Then don't take all day."

CHAPTER 15

Tom had decided to eat at Maybelle's. The food was as good as anywhere else, and he liked Maybelle. She wasn't there when he came in, but he was given a plate and told to help himself by an older woman who doubled on cooking and cleaning.

"She left when the dinner crowd was gone. She likes to go home and get her beauty nap before the supper hour. Just help yourself. I kept everything warm."

He got a plate, filled it with stew, tore off a chunk of bread, took himself a big piece of apple pie and poured a cup of coffee. He ate alone in the dining room, and sat back to enjoy himself. He wasn't going to get anything this good for supper.

Maybelle's was the fourth place Nate Lovelace approached. He looked in the door and saw a cowboy sitting there, eating. He stepped back out and took a good look up the street. There was no one coming. He went back in. He figured to make this short and sweet.

He stepped all the way into the dining room and Tom looked up. Nate said, "Are you Tom Cameron?"

"I think so." He didn't stop eating. "There's more on the stove. You're supposed to help yourself."

Nate felt better. There was no resemblance between this man and Morgan. This was strictly a cowboy. If they were going to try roping each other, he might stand a chance. The young man sitting there could probably work him under on a trail drive or a roundup, but he was thinking about drawing a gun, and *that* was Nate Lovelace's business.

He stepped close. "I'm Nate Lovelace."

"I figured that out. I think the gun gave you away."

"I understand you don't have one."

"They make too much noise."

"I brought one along." He walked over and put it on the table. "You can put it on or just draw it out now and hold it in your hand."

"I didn't eat my pie yet."

"I don't happen to have all day."

"I'm not really interested in things like this."

"I'm not asking you to make a career out of it. I just want you to do it once."

"My brother gets a kick out of these things. Why don't you wait for him?"

"I could simply shoot you and put the gun on you after I'm done."

"You wouldn't do that." Tom pushed his plate back. "That's one thing about people like you. You want the edge all the time, but you also want an alibi. You only want it to look fair."

Nate pulled his gun. "You're wrong." He fired. The bullet took a small piece of flesh from the edge of Tom's left shoulder. The cook and cleaning woman looked in and went right back out.

Nate said, "This is your last chance."

"Do you really want to do this?"

Nate returned the gun to the holster. "You got thirty seconds."

"How about the pie first?"

"Twenty seconds."

"All right, all right, I'll do it. Then I hope you'll be satisfied." He stood up, dabbing at the blood on his shoulder. "Damn, that stings."

He swung the gun belt around his waist smoothly and buckled it. He turned his back on Nate and slid the gun out once, hefting it, and put it back. Then he turned around and said, "Go ahead. I'm ready whenever you are."

For the briefest moment, Nate Lovelace had second thoughts. There was something familiar about the way Tom Cameron had moved. He saw now the resemblance between him and Morgan. It was the same mannerism that Morgan had, the same shift of weight, the same little twist of the wrist before putting the gun away. For the slightest of moments, Nate felt a touch of fear. Then he pushed it away. He concentrated. He put everything else out of his mind. He said, evenly, "You first."

Tom laughed. He shook his head, amazed. He said, "Did you ever," then drawing the gun, bringing it up level and firing, he continued, "think that you could make a mistake?"

Nate Lovelace didn't hear him. He had finally reacted to the movement but he was too late. He got his gun out but he never fired it. The bullet entered him dead center, straight into the heart. He was stunned when he fell. He died in less than two minutes.

When Morgan came into Calendar, he found Tom getting his horse from the blacksmith. Someone had already told him about Nate Lovelace.

Tom was not wearing a gun. He paid Jake Hoover and said to Morgan, "Did you come in to keep me company going back?"

"What the hell happened?"

"He underestimated me."

"Most people would have bet that way. He was very good. He was as good as his reputation."

"Shooting people is not that hard, Morgan. I'm not interested in it. I'd rather build up a herd and see a ranch grow and prosper. I'd rather do something constructive with my time. But if I wanted to shoot people, I could do it as well as the next person."

"Obviously."

Tom smiled. "Hey, I had a good teacher."

"Who?"

"Remember when you would take Pa's gun and sneak off and practice? I'd watch you, then I'd practice. I'd do exactly what you did. You'd put Pa's gun back and I'd get it out. When we were kids, all I ever wanted to be was just like you."

"You're crazy."

"I didn't think so then." He got up and rode past his brother and said, as they started out toward the street, "And I don't think so now."

CHAPTER 16

One of the Texans said to Floyd, "Why don't I ride over there and talk to him a minute?"

"What for?"

"Well, we've been at this for more'n an hour now, and we're not getting anywhere that I can see. It can't hurt to talk. It might help."

"I'll give you ten minutes. Don't take all day."

The Texan looked at him. "Don't do anything dumb while I'm out there."

He rode down off the hill and held both hands up in the air. He rode slowly. He suddenly wasn't crazy about the idea.

Reuben saw him coming. He watched everyone else. He kept the Sharps ready.

The rider started up the other side, toward the top of the hill where the wagon was. He had last shaved two days ago. He wore a battered hat he must have had a long time. He had a toothpick stuck in the side of his mouth.

Reuben finally said, "That's far enough."

The Texan thought, Jesus, that wagon's chewed up. Where the hell was he hiding while we pumped all that lead in there? He said, "Can I get down?"

"Leave your rifle on your horse."

He got down carefully and walked around the wagon. Reuben took a last look at the other side of the hill, then stood up.

The Texan looked at him, saw the blood, noticed how often he was hit, and thought, we're never going to get this man. He said, "I was sitting over there thinking, this whole thing is stupid."

Reuben said, "If I remember, this wasn't my idea."

"You wouldn't consider pulling out, would you?"

"I don't think I could do that."

"We'd give you time."

"I don't think so."

"Floyd's going to do something soon. He's as crazy as Dahlman but only half as smart. You got the man talking to himself."

"Tell him not to hang back the next time. Tell him to come on out where I can get a good look at him."

Reuben stood with his vest balled up and pressed against the bleeding in his chest. The Texan said, "Why don't you let me tie something around that right?"

"That's nice of you to offer, but I think I got the hang of it now."

"You lost a little blood."

"A little."

"You want a cigarette?"

"No, but I could use a chew."

The Texan fished a plug of tobacco out of his pocket, stepped up close, and held it while Reuben bit off the end.

"Thanks."

"You know you don't have a chance in hell. At first, Floyd was being careful. He thought it would be easy. Now he don't care if he loses everyone. He wants your neck, and he wants it bad."

Reuben looked at him. "I figure I can get at least five more no matter what you people do. I hope he's one of them. You could be one of those five, and then I don't think you'll care whether he gets me or not."

"You're right. I'm not too sure I care that much right now. See you around."

He got up on his horse and, without another look, rode back.

Floyd said, "Well?"

The Texan said, "I think you got your hands full."

"What did he say?"

"He wanted me to tell you not to hang back the next time."

"That son of a— Keller! Come here!"

One of the men walked his horse over.

"Take ten men. Go up through those trees. I want you to circle all the way around behind him. When you're in position, fire a shot. Then I'll fire a shot and we'll rush him from all sides. Let's go."

Keller nodded and rode off. He picked out ten men and they filed off the hill and headed toward the trees on the far side.

The Texan said to Floyd, "You're crazy. If we come at him front and back, we'll be shooting at each other."

"Just keep low."

"Keep low? I'm going home." He turned his horse and rode away.

Frank Cameron tested his leg a couple of times. It felt pretty good. So did he. He had gotten himself back in shape. It had come along faster than he had expected.

He pushed the horse. He tried to pace himself, but he wanted to make time. He tried not to think about Tom. There was nothing he could do about that right now. If Morgan got there in time, he knew it would be all right. Anyway, now he wanted to find Reuben. He didn't know how much time he had, so he pushed the horse a little more.

He had no trouble following the wagon tracks, and when he climbed the first hill he stopped to take a good look and let the horse stamp and blow a little. He thought he saw something but he couldn't be sure, so he swung down off the hill and headed for the next one.

This time he was sure he saw something, but he couldn't quite make it out. The horse was sweating pretty good and he hated to do it, but he forced the big brown down off the hill again and headed for the other side.

When he topped the last hill, he saw the wagon. It was turned over, two hills away. He immediately pushed the horse again. Finally, he saw Reuben, sitting with his back to the wagon, holding his Sharps. About thirty riders sat on the far hill, waiting. He saw some more riders moving off on one side, heading toward the trees.

Reuben had seen him coming for ten minutes now. At first, he wasn't too sure who it was; it didn't look like

Morgan or Tom. Then he remembered. When he was a boy, he had seen his pa ride like that. He had always thought there was no one who could get more out of a horse than his father. He watched him coming closer with each hill, and for the first time he thought he might make it.

Frank slowed down and let the horse walk the last hill. They went down slow and up the other side, and he slipped off the horse and walked beside him. Frank felt a lot better once he had seen Reuben and knew he was still alive. Once he knew that, he knew that anything else could be handled.

He left the horse with Reuben's. He loosened the cinch straps, got his rifle and walked up to the wagon.

"Reuben, did somebody object to you cutting down a few trees?"

"Well, they haven't been helping me load the wagon."

"What are you doing with your vest?"

"Plugging a hole."

"Let me see that."

"You're not going to use any of Doc Kruger's methods, are you?"

"No." He took a look at the wound. It had stopped bleeding. It was just seeping a little, and didn't look too bad. Reuben also had the tip of one finger blown off and a number of minor hits, so Frank went back and got some things out of his bedroll. He wrapped Reuben's ribs, patched him up and cleaned him off a little. Reuben kept his eyes on Floyd Walker while his father worked, and kept track of the progress of the riders moving through the trees.

Frank looked around. "You've been busy."

"Lucky, too. The one I'd like to get, though, is that one on that sorrel. That's Floyd Walker."

"I know Floyd."

"He won't come close enough for me to get a shot at him."

"Even with that big Sharps?"

"Yeah."

Frank took a look. "I figure he's sitting out there about seven hundred yards. Let me see that rifle."

Reuben handed it to him. "It's loaded."

"I had a friend who taught me a trick once with a Sharps." He sat down and rested the big barrel on the end of the wagon. He sighted a long time, looked up and said, "If the wind don't kick up, I think I can do it. You want him hit high or low?" He went back to sighting along the big barrel, barely breathing, and finally squeezed the trigger.

Floyd Walker sat without talking to anyone. He was steaming. When the Texan left, he almost turned and shot him in the back. He watched now for his men to circle the wagon and get into position.

He was so mad, and sat there brooding so much, he almost missed the lone rider approaching from the other direction.

"Who the hell is that?"

No one said anything. They watched the rider get

close, and finally get down and walk up to the wagon, carrying a rifle. Floyd was certain it was the old man. Now he had two of them. But one more was not going to make any difference. He had made up his mind. He was going to rush the wagon as soon as the other group was ready, no matter how many more showed up.

He rolled a cigarette, trying to calm down. Let's go, he thought. He stuck the cigarette in his mouth and struck a match along the side of his pants. He was just lighting the cigarette when the big .55 slug caught him flush in the chest. Even at that distance, it had enough velocity to knock him off his horse. The sound of the shot came late out over the valley.

The other riders pulled back, nervously. They looked at Floyd. He was not going to get up.

Someone said, "I think it's time to go home."

No one gave him any argument.

"What do we do now?" Reuben looked at his father.

They were alone. Everyone had pulled out. The riders up in the trees were called back and they all turned and rode away.

They turned the wagon over. It was in bad shape, but it would go.

Frank said, "We'll come back for it. We're not going to cut any more wood today."

"What are we going to do?"

"I'm going to go see Dahlman."

CHAPTER 17

Jim Dahlman spent the early part of the afternoon going over some books. He was planning on making some cattle purchases, and had been considering Texas stock for some time. Maybe this was it.

He was also planning on a trip in about six weeks to St. Louis. He had been approached about some railroad mergers and a position on the board of directors. Even though he had been burned before, he was tempted. He was far from satisfied with the wealth he had accumulated. He had barely gotten started as far as he was concerned. Someone had talked to him about buying property in San Francisco; someone else was over a barrel and might let some good properties go cheap. He was thinking about making a quick trip out there.

He was drinking a cup of coffee out of an old cup he had had around for years, and he knew he should get rid of some of his old ways—like the desk he was sitting at. He should bring in a new one now that shipping on the railroad was not that expensive, and get someone to come in and help him put up another house.

He had been impressed last summer in Omaha when he stayed a week with Clarence Knisely. That's the kind of house he should have. It gives you respect.

Red knocked in the doorway and waited. Dahlman motioned for him to come in. "Didn't you go with Floyd?"

"No. I was up along the creek this morning and didn't get back in time. But I ran into someone coming out of Calendar on my way back. He said Nate Lovelace is dead."

Dahlman turned all the way around. "Did he get anyone?"

"No. One of the Camerons got him."

"All right." He waved him off. He didn't show any emotion. He made a mental note—check with Floyd on the chances of getting Les Singletree from Waco.

He heard the riders come back, but he kept working. Soon he realized that no one had come in, and he wondered where Floyd was. He pushed the books aside and got up. He went to the door.

There wasn't anyone near the house. A wrangler was hitching up a large wagon near the corral.

"Hey!" Dahlman waved his hand. He put two fingers in his mouth and whistled. He yelled, "Come here."

The wrangler finished first, then walked over. He was wearing chaps and walked with a stiff-legged gait. He didn't wear a gun. He had been breaking horses for the Circle C for two years. He had a lot of savvy and Dahlman was pleased with him.

"Did Floyd come back?"

"No. I'm getting that wagon ready now to go get him."

"Where is he?"

"From what I've been told, he's about an hour from

here, laying flat on his back. That trapper put a hole in his chest with a Sharps."

"What the hell is going on here?"

"Floyd went and got himself killed. They jumped that trapper you were worried about so much out collecting firewood. He proved harder to take than Floyd thought. There are seventeen men out there. The rest came back. They don't seem like they're planning on going out again."

"Send someone up here. Get me Lennie or Bircher."

"I think Lennie and Bircher are both out there with Floyd."

"Get me someone. Is Jordan down there? Send him up."

The wrangler turned and walked away. A few minutes later, a cowboy came out of the bunkhouse and walked up toward the house. He was short and stocky and bald. He didn't seem anxious to come. Dahlman had dug a piece of cigar out of his pocket and got it burning. He tried to relax. He was sure Floyd had mishandled the whole damn thing. How hard is it to take fifty men and run four more off a two-bit spread? Christ, a woman could do it. He could have given the job to a nester, and he could have done it. The cook could have done it.

Jordan was not happy about trying to explain anything to Dahlman. He had been with him for eight years and knew what he was like. He had always been able to put up with it. He wasn't thinking about leaving like those damn Texans were fixing to do. He would like to stay on, so he wasn't happy about being put on the spot. He didn't want to have to explain what he couldn't believe himself. But he had been there. Each step had made sense at the time. It should have worked. The right shot here or there and there would be nothing to explain.

Dahlman said coldly, "What happened?"

"We came across one of the Camerons collecting firewood. He had just come out of the stand of timber the other side of the old trail. We had him out in the open, and Floyd tried to run over him. He took cover behind his wagon, opened fire with a Sharps and, hell, I don't think he missed a shot. We tried a couple of different things, but nothing seemed to work. Everybody was getting a little spooked. Then someone else came out from the ranch, I think it was the old man, and one of them got off a shot that hit Floyd. It must have carried close to eight hundred yards. When that happened, everybody decided to come on back."

"Tell them to get ready. I'll take them over there this time."

"I don't know, Mr. Dahlman. The Texans are leaving."

"Let them go. Get everybody else ready. I'll be down there in ten minutes."

"There's some more talking about going."

"Look, you tell whoever's staying to get ready. I don't care if it's only five. I'm going over to the Box C and finish what I started. I'm going over there if I have to go by myself."

"Yes, sir."

Dahlman got a gun and buckled it on. He took a Winchester off the wall in his bedroom and loaded it. His cigar had gone out, but he hadn't noticed.

He left the house. There were about fifteen men sad-
dling horses at the corral. He saw them suddenly stop.
Around the far corner of the stable came four riders,
holding their horses at a walk, heading straight for the
house.

When Frank and Reuben came up past Silver Springs
across the shallow creek headed toward the ranch build-
ings, they saw Morgan and Tom waiting.

Frank felt a tremendous relief. He almost felt good
enough to turn around and go back home.

Morgan said, "Do you mind a little company?"

Tom said, "What were you doing, Reuben? You look as
if a tree fell on you."

Morgan said, "Doc Kruger wasn't practicing medicine
on him, was he, Pa?"

"Leave your brother alone, he's had a trying day."

Reuben said, "It ain't easy to look like this. When we
get home, I'll show you how it's done."

Frank said, "Did you run into Lovelace, Morgan?"

"I got there too late. Tom had already taken care of it."

"Tom?"

"The boy is learning."

Tom said, "Are you going to have a talk with Mr.
Dahlman?"

"Something like that."

Morgan said, "It's about time."

Dahlman watched them come toward the house. The
one who looked like a young boy was off to the right. On
the other side was one who had a cold look. The one car-

rying the Sharps looked like hell. He was wrapped around the chest, had a livid mark across his face, and his arms were patched. He didn't act as if he were ready for bed, though. Dahlman looked at the one in front. That couldn't be the same man he had burned out and shot in the leg. This man didn't look like he would let anyone burn him out.

The men at the corral spread out a little. They stayed alert, but made no move to come up near the house. Dahlman stood out from under the low porch roof and waited. They were now about fifty yards away. Red came out and stood near the corner of the house.

Frank Cameron stopped his horse when he got within twenty feet. He said, "I understand you wanted to see me."

"When I want to see you, I'll let you know."

"Dahlman, you burned me out once, but you're never going to do that again."

"Maybe."

"No. You don't understand me. It's going to be you or me, once and for all. And it's going to be done right now."

Dahlman looked at Frank Cameron and knew he couldn't do it. It was a shock. He was not going to be able to pull his gun. Had he changed that much? It had been a long time since he faced anyone without all the power his money gave him at his side.

He looked at Frank some more and didn't think he could beat him. And he didn't want to take the chance. He would stall him somehow, and get him another way. That's what he had money for, to make it possible to have things done without running a personal risk. He looked at

Frank Cameron, knew he was going to back down, and
suddenly he hated him passionately.

"Dahlman. Now."

"No. You got a complaint, go talk to the sheriff."

"My complaint is you. You shoot people in the back,
and you jump them late at night. You shoot them from
the brush. You murder people who never bother you. You
do it because they're weak or small or unable to protect
themselves. You do it that way because you have no guts.
You don't have a ranch here; you have a cesspool. You lie,
you cheat, you steal, you murder, and you don't have the
guts to do it out in the open. Pull your gun. Pull your gun
or I'll shoot you in the goddamn leg."

"No."

Frank Cameron waited a long moment. Finally, in dis-
gust, he said, "You make me sick."

Morgan said, "Pa, you've got to shoot him."

"I can't do that."

"You've got to. You can't let him go now."

"I can't. There's a difference between him and me."

"Then I'll do it."

"No!" Frank turned. "No."

Tom said, softly, "Morgan's right, Pa. It's got to be
done."

Frank turned his horse around and faced his sons. "No.
I didn't bring you up to do something like this." He motioned with his hand. "We'll go home. He'll make a mistake. All we have to do is wait."

Reuben said, "I agree with them, Pa. I think you're
wrong. If you weren't here, I'd just shoot him. But if you

want us to go home, we'll go home." He turned his horse.

Tom turned his horse reluctantly. Morgan waited a long moment and then finally turned his. They started back out.

Jim Dahlman pulled his gun, aimed it deliberately, and fired. He shot Frank Cameron in the back.

He thought all he had to do was kill the father. He thought there would be sudden confusion; they would be stunned, upset, leaderless, and panic. He thought Red would fire, too. He thought the men at the corral would open fire once he did. The others would be caught and cut down. Actually, when he first pulled his gun, he wasn't thinking at all. He was blind with rage.

He never had the chance to realize he was wrong. The shot was no sooner off than the other three whirled at the sound and fired, almost simultaneously. Morgan was a trifle faster, but Reuben and Tom were a close second. The heavy slug from the Sharps and the slugs from the two .44's drove him flat against the front of the house. He fell over onto his face.

No one else moved. Red turned and walked away. The others went back inside the bunkhouse.

Frank managed to stay on his horse. He held on fast, though the breath was knocked out of him. Tom reached him first. He grabbed Tom's arm and held on. He said, "Tom?"

"What?"

He leaned over, barely able to talk, and said, "Don't take me to Doc Kruger." He looked up and half-smiled. "Keep that old coot away from me."

CHAPTER 18

It was three days before Frank Cameron realized he was in his own house. He kept moving in and out of consciousness, running a high temperature, seeing Tia leaning over him, and imagining he was back in the dugout. Then it all cleared up and he opened his eyes and knew he was home.

He opened his eyes and looked straight into Tia's. She said, "You never came back for your shirt."

"It's good I didn't leave my pants there."

"I brought it with me."

"That's good because I don't want you to go back."

Doc Kruger was sitting at the kitchen table. He got up and walked into the bedroom. "Is he finally awake?" He leaned down and said, "Tom told me the first thing you said was go get Doc Kruger."

"That boy never did get anything straight."

"You lost a lung. It may cut down on your singing, but that's about all."

"Dahlman?"

"He had a beautiful funeral."

"My boys?"

"They're all around here somewhere."

"Tell them to keep busy. I want things done when I get up."

Two weeks later, it started. Frank knew it would. He knew it was something he couldn't stop.

Morgan was the first. He said, "I think I'll leave tomorrow."

Frank was walking pretty good by that time. Tia had moved in. The bandages were off. He could take a deep breath without any pain. He was planning on doing some riding by the end of the week.

Morgan said, "There's a stagecoach I'm planning on taking. It goes past a place called Three Trees. I'd like to get there before cold weather."

Frank said, "I think I can do this, Morgan, if you promise to come back just once. If I had that to look forward to, if I knew I'd see you again sometime, I could do this now without acting like a fool."

"It's a promise."

Reuben simply got his stuff together, saddled his horse, and said, "I don't need no speech. I'll come back sometime. At least once."

Frank said, "Reuben, I don't want you to leave here thinking your father is over the hill. Remember what we used to do when you were a kid. Well, I can still take you two falls out of three." And he suddenly grabbed him around the waist.

Reuben tried to hold back. "Take it easy. You'll hurt yourself."

Frank pulled him until the two of them went off their feet, Reuben trying not to use his strength, and they rolled over once.

Reuben lay back and said, "What are you trying to do?"

Frank put his face on his son's chest for a moment and then looked at him and said, "I'm trying to say goodbye."

Tom was the last one. He waited almost a week longer, until his father was riding pretty good.

Frank came up from the stable early in the evening. Tom was waiting at the house, and he said, "I guess I'll go tomorrow."

Frank said, "I've been thinking. Why don't I put this ranch in your name and you stay right here? You're a rancher. You know more about cows than anybody I know. This is a ranch again. Why work for someone else? Stay right here and build up the place. We've got grass and good stock and plenty of room."

"I can't do that."

"Why not?"

"I can't take your ranch away from you."

"All right, I've been thinking again. How about partners? We'll put it in both names."

"I don't know."

"What's wrong with that?"

"It's not just me. There's two of us." He pointed to the door. The young girl who stayed with the woman stood there.

Frank said, "Hell, she don't eat that much."

Tom turned and walked away.

"Where are you going?"

"To unpack."

X